The Stevens Get Even

Adapted by Scott Ciencin
Based on the teleplay written by
Marc Warren and Dennis Rinsler
Based on characters created by
Matt Dearborn

Watch it on

New York

Chapter 1

The mastermind's fingers blurred across his computer keyboard. On his monitor, hundreds of digital images flew past.

For days, he'd been searching through countless family photos. Now it came down to a final few. He moved the computer cursor to the picture of the Stevens family. With one click, their faces filled the screen: a father, a mother, two sons, and a daughter. . . .

The mastermind's eyes widened. *This* was the family. He knew it.

Leaning back in his leather chair, the mastermind smiled. Then he whispered one word: "Perfect."

At that same moment, a much younger mastermind lurked in the bushes outside Lawrence Junior High.

Graduation Day had finally come. Teachers lined the stage and a lovely young woman in a cap and gown sang the school song from the podium.

In the audience, students joined in as she belted out the last lines of their alma mater: "And to thee—your Wombat whiskers we'll e'er be true!"

Applause followed, and Principal Wexler took the podium. "Ruby Mendel!" he cried joyously. "Thank you. Our beloved alma mater never sounded lovelier."

Ruby skipped off stage. Her pals, Ren and Monique, greeted her with excited hugs.

"Omigosh, guys," said the willowy Ren Stevens. "I'm going to miss you so much."

Monique smiled. "But, Ren, we'll be together in high school," she said.

"I know, I'm just a little . . ." Ren faltered, overcome by emotion.

"I know," Ruby said, and the friends hugged again.

From the stage, Principal Wexler continued. "Please welcome a student whose accomplishments are almost too numerous to mention. Anchor of the Wombat Report, president of the Overachievers Club, my personal assistant, and the single most amazing young woman I have ever met. . . . Good *gravy*, I'm going to miss her. Your valedictorian—Ren Stevens!"

The crowd of students and parents applauded once again. Only one graduate was silent. Larry Beale, Ren's longtime nemesis, sulked in his chair.

"Oh, Principal Wexler!" Ren exclaimed as she took the stage and hugged her mentor. "Thank you!"

Wexler sat down, dabbing his eyes with a handkerchief, and Ren began her address.

"Good afternoon, teachers, parents, and fellow graduates," she said. "Lawrence Junior High was not just a school, but it was a home away from home . . ."

In the warm sunlight, the smiling Ren glowed with happiness. In the shade of the bushes, however, her brother, Louis Stevens, could barely restrain his laughter—because this young mastermind knew what was coming next.

From the audience, Mr. and Mrs. Stevens beamed with pride as they watched their daughter, Ren.

"It was a place to learn, a place to play, a place to think, a place to grow . . ." she continued in her speech.

Mr. Stevens was so focused on his daughter, he didn't even notice *who* had just slid into the seat next to him.

"That's my little girl up there," whispered Mr. Stevens, nudging his new neighbor.

"I *know*, Dad," said Donnie Stevens. *Duh!* he thought. "I'm her brother."

Mr. Stevens whirled around in his chair. "Donnie!" he whispered. "You're *late*."

Donnie Stevens was the oldest child in the family. He was also a top jock, a star football player, and he'd also just graduated—from high school.

"Where's Louis?" Mrs. Stevens asked him. "He's going to miss Ren's speech."

"I dropped him and Beans off," Donnie told them. "He said he wanted a better angle."

Concern crossed Mr. Stevens's features. "For what?" he asked.

Donnie had no idea. And that's what worried Mr. Stevens the most.

Louis Stevens and his young friend and accomplice, Beans, scrambled to a new hiding place off to one side of the stage.

With shiny electronic gear on his head and a remote-control device in his hand, Louis looked like a walking human video game.

He peered at the stage through binoculars. At the podium, his sister droned on: "We were tiny tadpoles in a pond of knowledge . . ."

"Ready to launch, boss?" Beans asked eagerly.

"Patience, Beans," Louis replied, then got to work.

"And even as we look to our future, we'll never forget our past," Ren continued forcefully.

"Wherever we go on this great planet I like to call . . . Earth—" she gave a little chuckle— "we'll keep the Wombat spirit alive in our . . ."

Suddenly, Ren noticed something floating— yes, *floating*—past her face. *No*, she thought, it can't be . . . but it was . . . a *beach ball*.

The colorful plastic ball began to bounce crazily around her. In the audience, students laughed and pointed.

Refusing to be distracted, Ren went on. "What is the Wombat spirit? Good question. It is service, dedication . . ."

The beach ball bopped Principal Wexler in the face. Angrily, the plump man called to one of the teachers. "Coach Tugnut! Confiscate that beach ball!"

"I'm on it, chief!" Tugnut cried. The coach tried to snag the beach ball, but it jerked around so much, he ended up flopping off the stage.

The audience burst into laughter!

From their hiding place, Louis and Beans giggled as they watched Tugnut flailing miserably in his attempts to snag their bobbing remote-controlled beach ball.

Gritting her teeth, Ren flipped through her notes and forged ahead, trying to ignore the crazy ball. "We'll keep the Wombat spirit alive in our hearts," she continued.

In the audience, Larry Beale laughed and pointed at Ren as the beach ball beaned her. Annoyed, she batted it away.

Beans reached for the remote. "Lemme play with that!" he cried.

"Beans, stop it!" warned Louis as he worked the controls. "This is not a toy, all right? This is my job. *This* is what I do."

"And sure it's easy to say, me, me, *me*. . . ." Ren flinched as the beach ball banged the back of her head. "But what about we, we, we—"

Coach Tugnut tried to come to Ren's rescue. But the beach ball suddenly veered away. Now, it was floating above the audience. The frustrated coach lunged after it again.

Ren tried to go on. "Remember, there is no 'I' in Wombat," she proudly declared. Then a loud cheer erupted from the crowd—that had more to do with the beach ball game than Ren's sage advice—and she surrendered, tossing the rest of her speech cards into the air. "Thank you," she concluded.

As sparse applause followed, Louis licked his trigger finger. "Time to release the confetti," he announced as he pressed a button.

"*Confetti?*" Beans asked in confusion. "I thought you said—"

Suddenly, the beach ball burst open— showering Coach Tugnut in pasta and tomato sauce. The sprayed audience scrambled away, shouting and shrieking.

"—spaghetti!" Beans informed Louis.

Ren fumed as she wiped spots of sauce from her face.

Louis's eyes widened in surprise and then pure diabolical delight. "Beans," he said, "your lack of listening skills finally paid off!"

In the audience, Tugnut slurped strands of pasta off his face. Ren, on the other hand, began to scan the area for the guilty party. When she spotted Louis and Beans, she shot them a look that said one thing: *you are so busted*!

Gulping, Louis murmured, "Beans, I think we should lie low for a while. All right?"

But when he turned, Beans had magically disappeared. "*Beans?*" he croaked.

Ren's rage was radical as she shoved up the sleeves of her ruined yellow graduation robe and raced toward her younger brother.

Louis took one look at his enraged sister and tore off through the bushes. He didn't consider himself a chicken, but he saw no reason why he should wait around for Ren to rearrange his face!

Ten minutes later, it was Principal Wexler who caught up to Louis in the school parking lot. Immediately, the big man put the boy in a wrestling headlock and pulled him back through the crowd of parents and students.

"Mr. Wexler," Louis gasped from his half-bent position. "You *can't* give me detention. It's summer vacation, sir. Please!"

When Wexler reached the rest of the Stevens family, he released Louis. "Rats, you're right," he told him. Then he brightened. "But *think* of all the days you'll owe me next year." And with a final glance at Mr. and Mrs. Stevens, Wexler said, "He's all yours."

The entire Stevens family stared at Louis.

"*What?*" Louis asked.

"Oh, I'll *show* you what!" Ren shouted, lunging for her brother's throat. Donnie seized her around the waist and pulled her back.

"Whoa!" Donnie cried, careful of his sister's kicks.

Louis pointed at his older sister. "She's crazy!" he cried.

"*Enough!*" their mother hollered angrily. "This is a *happy* day! We should all be *happy!*"

Everyone stared at Mrs. Stevens. "Don't you guys realize that Donnie's going off to college in the fall?" she told them. "And Ren will be starting high school. . . . Soon you'll *all* be leaving home. Out on your own."

The kids glanced sheepishly at each other.

"This is a precious time," Mrs. Stevens pointed out. "We should make the most of this summer."

"Mom's right, guys," Donnie told them. "We need to cherish these days together. But . . . I've got a date, so, first thing tomorrow, there's going to be some *serious* cherishing. Bye!"

10

With a wave, Donnie fled.

Louis backed away. "Yeah, uh—I gotta meet up with the guys. So, cherish ya later!" He zipped off.

Mr. Stevens looked forlorn. "Guess it's just the three of us," he said to Ren and Mrs. Stevens.

Ren raised an eyebrow. "Um, actually," she confessed, "Gil's taking me out to dinner."

"Gil?" asked Mr. Stevens, perplexed.

Frowning, Ren said, "He's only been my boyfriend for the past *three months*, Dad."

Mr. Stevens shook his head. "Doesn't ring a bell," he admitted.

Ren's mother sighed. "Your father's still in denial," she said. "Go. Have a good time."

"Thanks," Ren said. "I love you guys."

Then Ren ran off before her parents could even kiss her good-bye. She didn't even notice Coach Tugnut, racing in a panic through the crowd, hungry birds diving down for a taste of the spaghetti on his head!

Chapter 2

Ren met up with her boyfriend at Roller Cakes, a fifties-style diner that featured pancakes served by waitresses on roller skates.

As a busy waitress zoomed past their booth, Gil spun the lazy Susan of pancake syrups. For some reason, he seemed more interested in the syrups than in Ren.

"Gil, we are going to have such a great summer," Ren said brightly. She could see he was in a bad mood, and she was determined to cheer him up. "We can spend every day together!"

"Can you believe how many syrups they have?" Gil asked, continuing to spin the lazy Susan.

"Hey, are you okay?" she asked.

Gil looked up. "Yeah, fine. It's just that, well . . . I took a summer job at a camp," he told her. "I'm going to teach swimming to little kids."

"Oh," Ren said, a little disappointed. "Well, that's great. We'll have nights and weekends."

"Ren, it's not a day camp," he said flatly.

"Oh," she said again. "Okay."

"It's in *Maine*," he finally confessed.

"Oh, yeah?" Ren said, her voice no longer bright. There was no getting around this news— it was bad. "That's really far," she murmured.

"I know," he said. "I'm sorry."

"It's okay," Ren assured him, trying to rally. After all, they could talk on the phone and write letters. "I'm gonna miss you so much."

"Yeah," Gil said.

Ren stared at Gil and waited. "*Yeah?*" she repeated. "That's *usually* where people say, 'I'm going to miss you too.'"

"Ren, here's the thing. . . ." Gil began.

"Uh-oh," muttered Ren.

"I mean, it's been great," Gil told her, "but I'm going away and I don't want to be tied down."

"Oh, sure," Ren said calmly. "In case you meet another girl."

He leaned back. "Well . . . I *probably* won't," he said.

"I know." Ren struggled to keep her voice level. "But when you're in Maine, you want to keep your options open."

"Right! Exactly," Gil said. He finally relaxed, thinking she would be totally fine with his plan. "When I come back, we can pick things up again."

"No, Gil," Ren snapped. "We can't."

"Ren. Are you upset?" he asked, perplexed.

"You dump me in a pancake house and you wonder if I'm upset!" she exclaimed. Jumping to her feet, she grabbed one of the syrups off the lazy Susan and held it over Gil's head.

Nothing came out.

"This would be a great moment if this syrup wasn't so thick!" she cried. Then, slamming down the dispenser, she ran out.

14

* * *

When Ren came through the front door, she found her mother reading on the living room couch.

Looking up from her book, her mother said, "Hi, honey. How was your dinner with Gil?"

All the way home, Ren had told herself that Gil was a jerk. That he didn't matter. She'd always been a girl in control—and she vowed to stay that way. But when Ren looked into her mother's face, she lost it. "Oh, Mom . . ." she said.

Dropping to the couch, Ren fell into her mother's arms and began to cry.

The next morning dawned bright and clear. School was finally over, and the summer sun bathed the Stevenses' house in a golden glow.

To begin the first of many lazy days ahead, Louis retired to the backyard. He had just put the finishing touches on his latest invention: the Ultra-Lounge-O-Matic Super Chair. Basically, it was a plastic lawn chair that he'd rigged with all sorts of gadgetry.

Around noon, his friends gathered to check it out.

"The technology is amazing," appraised Louis's geeky friend Tom Gribalski.

The always-cool Alan Twitty agreed. "It's your masterpiece," he declared.

Pretty Tawny Dean crossed her arms over her chest. "You're *really* going to sit in this thing all summer?" she asked.

"Hold on, hold on!" Louis cried from the chair. "Don't call her a *thing*. She's my Ultra-Lounge-O-Matic Super Chair."

Louis tapped a button on his chair and a mechanical hand presented him with a can of soda.

Twitty grinned. "Sweet!" he cried.

Louis settled back. "Watch this. Watch this." He hit another button and the chair *vibrated*. "Like a thousand tiny fingers workin' all the good parts!"

Tawny rolled her eyes. "You've brought laziness to an art form," she told him.

Louis selected yet another button. A mechanical voice said, "Thank you, Tawny."

"Well, it certainly looks like it has all the bells and whistles," Tom said with a geeky grin of appreciation.

"That reminds me. . . ." Louis struck another button and settled back with a flourish. "Snack time!" One mechanical arm delivered a hot dog, while another spread mustard on it and held it under Louis's mouth.

As he took a bite, Twitty stared with envy while Tawny stared with disgust.

Louis crowed, "Oh, and for my entertainment pleasure . . ." A TV screen popped up between his feet.

A show called *Gotcha!*—starring Lance Lebow—had just started. As the volume rose, everyone gathered around.

Meanwhile, inside the Stevenses' house, Ren bounded down the stairs and into the kitchen.

"Good morning!" she called to her parents. "Hey, Dad, come and give me a kiss."

He did. Then Ren planted one on her mom's cheek. "Hey, Mom, how are you *doin'*?!" she chirped like a cheerleader.

Mr. and Mrs. Stevens shared a concerned look. Ren's mother turned to her. "You doin' okay, honey?" she asked.

"I'm fine. I'm *great*," Ren said firmly. "Super. Tip-top. Never better." She grinned. "Do you think I'm going to let some *boy* ruin my summer? Nuh-uh."

Ren's father smiled with relief. "So you're really over what's his name?" he asked.

Ren blinked, then crumbled. "His name is Gil. Gil. *Gil!*" she sobbed.

Ren's mother passed her daughter a napkin. "Oh, no, honey," she said. "It's okay."

Mr. Stevens stared, horrified. "This looks like one of those mother-daughter conversations," he said. Then he rushed out of the room.

Passing by Mr. Stevens, Beans ambled into the kitchen, pulling a suitcase on wheels. "So, where will I be bunking?" the little boy asked brightly.

Beans didn't seem to notice he'd just entered Heartbreak Hotel.

As Ren's sobbing subsided, Mrs. Stevens looked up. "*Bunking?*" she asked.

With a sniffle, Ren explained, "Yeah, Mom, I took a babysitting job to get my mind off you-know-who."

"Oh," Mrs. Stevens said.

Ren noticed the suitcase. "Hey, Beans," she said, "you *know* I'm just watching you for the afternoon."

"I don't think my parents will appreciate that," he said.

"Why not?" Ren asked.

"They're in Helsinki," he told her.

"Helsinki?" cried Ren and her mother together.

"It's in Finland." Beans shrugged. "Get a globe." He picked up a spoon from the sink and sniffed it. "Mmmm—*someone* had rice pudding."

Mrs. Stevens shuddered. The family had held long discussions about Beans's true origins. Animal? Vegetable? Mineral? The jury was still out.

"Uh, Beansy. Honey. Little guy. *Put it down!*" Mrs. Stevens commanded. The spoon dropped back in the sink. "So, Beansy," Mrs. Stevens continued, "I just don't think this is a great idea. Really, how long will your parents be away?"

"Two weeks," Beans replied. "Three, tops."

"Three, tops? *Three?*" she cried.

Beans pulled his suitcase over to the refrigerator. "Time to unpack!" he declared.

"Beans, the guest room is *upstairs*," said Ren.

"You think I don't *know* that?" he said as he opened the case. It was filled with bacon strips.

"You brought your own bacon?" asked Ren, horrified.

"No, I'm holding it for a friend," Beans said sarcastically. "Ya want some?"

"Mom—*two weeks* of Beans," Ren murmured, looking queasy.

"Three, *tops*," Beans said, and he began to load his bacon into the refrigerator.

In the backyard, Louis and his friends remained glued to *Gotcha!* On the TV screen, a waiter announced, "The specialty of the house!"

Sitting around a café table, a family watched the waiter remove the cover on a large tray.

Underneath was a growling gorilla's head! The family jumped back and screamed in terror.

The gorilla beneath the table leaped up, bursting through the top. Then the gorilla tore his mask away to expose the face of the show's host—Lance Lebow.

"*Gotcha!*" Lance cried. "And, Van Gundy family, we 'Gotcha!' good!"

Sitting in his Ultra-Lounge-O-Matic Super Chair, Louis clicked off the TV and settled back, laughing. "That's so cold," he said, "yet so entertaining."

"Yeah, well, I've got to get rolling," said Twitty, "so, have a good . . . sit."

"Later, see you around," Louis called as Twitty took off. With a sly smile, he set his sights on pretty Tawny.

"Oh, *Tawny!*" Louis called. "I've got a little surprise for you."

Louis pulled a switch, releasing a small, foldout seat next to the main chair. With a wink, he patted the seat. "That's *your* seat," he told her. "Right next to Poppa."

"Actually, 'Poppa,' I've got to get home," said Tawny. With a roll of her eyes, she was outie.

"Oh, all right. Maybe tomorrow then!" Louis called after her. "I'll be here all summer!"

A buzzing sound suddenly whipped past Louis's ear. He slapped at the mosquito, smashing it against his neck. "Mosquitoes . . ." Louis murmured, an idea forming. "Hmmm . . ."

Later that afternoon, Ren strolled into her bedroom and found a disaster area!

Wearing a pair of her panty hose on his head, Beans was rifling through her dresser drawers, throwing clothing to the floor.

"Beans!" Ren yelped. "Get out of my stuff!"

"Don't worry," said the little boy. "They're not for me. Louis needed more mosquito netting for his chair."

Ren's nostrils flared. "*More,*" she repeated.

Storming downstairs and out the back door, Ren found Louis in his chair. He'd tented it with "mosquito netting" sewn together from her panty hose.

With a shriek of rage, Ren shredded the netting and glared in at him.

"Oh, come on, Ren," he complained. "You're letting in the 'skeeters!"

Ren just stood there, fists clenched, seething.

"Ren, can you just say something?" asked Louis. "'Cause that sick look is really startin' to freak me out."

"Wait'll I get my hands on you!" she screeched.

Louis darted from the chair just as Ren lunged for him. She ended up facedown on the seat. "Ow!" Ren wailed as a mechanical hand smacked her behind.

She struggled to get free—but a mechanical arm now had her trapped. "Get me out of this thing!" she cried.

"Press the red button!" yelled Louis.

Ren flailed her arms desperately. She hit a button at random and a stream of whipped cream and chocolate syrup squirted her in the face.

"Hey—the sundae maker works!" Louis said with a surprised grin. An arm came out and plopped a cherry on Ren's whipped-cream-covered head.

"That's it!" Ren pressed every single button she could find!

"I wouldn't do that," Louis warned.

The chair spun wildly. Ren shrieked. *"Mommy . . . !"* The chair hurled her forward. She hit the ground hard and lay sprawled at Louis's feet.

Louis gave her a weak smile and tried to think of something positive to say. "Wow, Ren," he said, "you really stuck that landing."

Ren jumped up and charged him like a mad bull going for a red cape. Louis ran.

Glancing backward, he noticed something even more dangerous than his big sister speeding his way. The Lounge-O-Matic was now chasing them both!

Chapter 3

At that very moment, a professional-looking gentleman strolled up the Stevenses' driveway. His name was Miles McDermott, and in some circles, he was considered a *mastermind*.

"Hello!" Miles called. "Anybody home?"

Louis and Ren raced across the lawn and crashed into Miles. All three went down. The crazed chair rocketed past them and smashed into a garden wall.

Ren and Louis scrambled to their feet and helped the stranger up. "Sir?" Ren cried, aghast. "Sir, are you all right? I am *so* sorry."

Mr. Stevens rushed over. "What's going on out here?" he asked.

"Ren freaked out and totally lost control!" Louis cried. "I had nothing to do with it."

"*Me?*" Ren replied. "Dad, look at me right now. He is destroying my life!"

"Who are you going to believe?" Louis whined. "Me! Your son!"

"Stop it!" Mr. Stevens demanded. "Would the two of you get along for five minutes, please?" He turned to the stranger. "Sir, are you okay?" he asked.

Miles dusted himself off. "Yes, I'm fine," he said.

"Good," Mr. Stevens said. "Well, if there's anything we can do, I'm happy—"

"Well, actually, you *can* help me," Miles told him. "I'm trying to find the Stevens family."

"We're the Stevens family," he said.

"You must be Steve!" Miles exclaimed, extending his hand. "Hi. Miles McDermott."

Mr. Stevens shook the man's hand. "Nice to meet you," he said.

"I have a little presentation for you," said Miles.

Mr. Stevens dropped his hand. "Oh, well, uh, Miles," he said, "whatever you're selling, we're really not interested."

Miles flinched. "Steve, you know, I'm not really a lawsuit kind of guy, but suddenly my back *is* feeling a little tight," he threatened.

Forcing a smile, Mr. Stevens led the way into the house. Mrs. Stevens and Donnie joined the others in the living room as Miles set up a screen and laptop projector.

"Stevens family," Miles began, "you have won an all-expense-paid vacation to the beautiful island paradise of—Mandelino!"

If it had been night, the crickets would have been the only sound in the room. *No one* reacted.

"Try to contain your enthusiasm," Miles told them.

Mrs. Stevens cleared her throat. "Miles, I have never *heard* of Mandelino," she said.

"Not surprising," Miles told her. He tapped some of the keys on his laptop to start a slick video presentation.

On the screen, a beautiful island sunset

appeared and the sultry voice of a woman began to narrate: "Mandelino is an uncharted, unspoiled island paradise. . . . Mandelino is populated by the descendents of island natives and shipwrecked sailors from many nations, making for the unique and varied look of its people."

Happy islanders of various races waved and smiled amidst images of the lush, tropical island.

"English is the mother tongue of Mandelino," the narrator continued, "so there'll be no language barrier as you experience the natural beauty and amazing Mandelinian hospitality never before offered to an outsider. Mandelino, your *dream* vacation!"

"Miles, it's all very interesting," said Mrs. Stevens, "but why us?"

"Well, you're an influential family here in Sacramento," Miles told her. "You're a state senator. Your husband works for a prominent law firm—"

"Actually," Mr. Stevens admitted, "I'm *between* prominent firms right now."

"I'm sorry to hear that," Miles said. "At any

rate, my company was hired to conduct an extensive search and you are exactly the family we're looking for . . . for this amazing opportunity."

Mr. Stevens shook his head. "Miles," he said, "I hate to be a Negative Ned, but what's the catch?"

Miles laughed. "There *is* no catch. We're just trying to get tourists to come to this island. All we ask is that you give us your honest opinion at the end of the trip—and allow us to quote you in our brochures."

"And that's it?" asked Mr. Stevens.

"Just sign on the dotted line!" exclaimed Miles. He placed a pen and piece of paper onto the coffee table.

"Dad, what are you waiting for?" asked Ren.

"Whoa—hold on!" Louis hollered. He had his summer plans all laid out, and they did *not* involve flying off to some island. He circled his sister. "Okay. You *know* this is boring," he told Ren. "You just want to go because you broke up with your stupid boyfriend and you want to get away!"

"And you just want to stay here and sit on your stupid chair," Ren countered.

"Do they have cable?" Donnie asked.

"Son," Miles replied, "the beauty of Mandelino is that there is no modern convenience of any kind."

"Guys, this sounds kinda cool," Donnie admitted. "I could run on the beach. Get into football shape."

"Donnie, *come on!*" Louis yelled, desperate now. "You can run *here* and get in shape *here!*"

"This could be a wonderful family adventure," Mrs. Stevens said, completely ignoring her youngest son. "It could be everything we've been hoping for."

"No, Mom, listen!" Louis moaned. "Here's an adventure: you can stay here and give me breakfast and do my laundry, and that'll be an adventure."

But his mother didn't seem to be listening.

"Dad, come on, *listen*," Louis continued, falling to his knees. "Somebody put a stop to the madness!"

"Well, I guess it's unanimous," Mr. Stevens chirped brightly. "We're going to Mandelino!"

"Yes!" Donnie and Ren shouted.

"Excellent," Miles said, his smile broadening.

"I guess we'd better start packing," said Mrs. Stevens. "We don't want to forget anything."

Beans suddenly appeared and plopped himself onto the arm of the couch. "Especially me!" he cried.

While Mrs. Stevens gasped, remembering their unexpected guest, Mr. Stevens scrawled his name on the contract. He felt very good about this vacation. For the first time since he'd lost his job, he was able to do something really nice for his family!

Sunlight sparkled like diamonds upon the ocean as the seaplane carrying Miles and the Stevens family soared past a lush, tropical island.

Miles pointed out the window. "If you look out on your right side, you'll see the beautiful island of Mandelino!" he announced.

Everyone crowded to the right-hand

31

windows—and the plane tilted drastically. "Not all at once!" Miles yelled.

Soon the seaplane glided across the water and stopped near the shore. The Stevens family emerged from the plane and took in the island paradise.

The people of Mandelino had crowded the beach to wave hello. More islanders sat in colorful canoes. Village drummers beat out a welcoming rhythm.

"Look at this!" Mrs. Stevens squealed excitedly as two well-built island men carried her from the seaplane's door to the beach's sand.

A group of enthusiastic islanders began to chant, "Welcome, Stevens family! Welcome, Stevens family!"

"Is this all for us?" Mrs. Stevens asked Miles.

"I think it *is*," answered the amazed Donnie.

The chanting flared in intensity as the family approached a group of villagers wearing colorful ceremonial robes. The barrel-chested leader raised his hand and the chanting instantly ceased.

"I am Tuka, chief elder of Mandelino," the big man proclaimed. "Welcome, Stevens family!" Tilting back his head, he blew into a ceremonial conch shell.

"This is very exciting," Miles said to the family.

"Yes, it *is*," Mr. Stevens agreed confidently. Then he frowned in confusion and asked, "Why?"

"You're about to be presented with the traditional Mandelino Hat of Friendship," Miles told him.

Excited islanders swarmed the family. Everyone received a hat that looked like the top of a pineapple with a chinstrap. Then they were each embraced.

Mrs. Stevens was hugged by a handsome, muscular young man. A little old lady grabbed Louis. A short, strong guy picked up Mr. Stevens and spun him around. And Beans was embraced by a beautiful young woman. He held on so tightly, Donnie practically had to pry the kid loose!

A handsome young man came forward to

hug Ren. He was about her age, with bronzed skin and golden hair. He was *such* a hottie, Ren had to force herself not to blush. "Welcome," the young man told Ren. "I am Mootai."

Ren's heart fluttered as she met the islander's gaze. Mootai was *so* good-looking and there was something *amazing* in his ocean-blue eyes.

Chemistry? thought Ren. Oh, yeah! But after Mootai hugged her, she simply held out her hand as if she were on a job interview. "My name is Ren," she said crisply, then she shook Mootai's hand as if he'd just sold her some insurance.

"Now come on," said Miles. "I'll show you where you'll be living."

Still wearing their festive pineapple hats, the Stevens family followed Miles as a few friendly islanders carried their luggage.

Miles led them to a beautiful house with a thatched roof and wraparound porch. It looked like a tropical mansion, and the family stared at it in awe.

"It's *magnificent*!" Mr. Stevens said.

"It's the palace of Tuka, the chief elder,"

Miles informed him. "They haven't built hotels yet, so he's allowing you to stay here as his guests."

Louis gripped Miles's shoulder. "Could I have one of the front rooms?" he begged. "I get nauseous if I don't have a spectacular ocean view."

Miles nodded, and Louis ran to the house.

"Wait!" Ren hollered, racing after him. "Oh, no. No, no, no, no!"

Chapter 4

Louis took in the sprawling, luxuriously decorated porch with wonder. "*Whoa . . .*" he murmured.

"Wait, wait, wait!" Ren yelled as she reached the porch steps. "Why does *he* get to have the room with a view?"

Louis raced inside Tuka's palace, Ren right at his heels. They stopped to admire the spacious living room, with its high ceiling, plush bamboo furniture, and local artifacts.

"This is *awesome*," Ren declared.

"Yeah," agreed Louis as he looked around through a telescope he'd snatched from a table. "I see *my* room."

Louis ran to a room marked Royal Bedroom.

"Oh, *no*," Ren warned. They reached the doorway at the same time, each trying to push the other aside.

"I called it," Louis growled as he shoved her. She pushed back. "No, you don't!"

"I *called* it!" He frowned. They weren't getting anywhere. But the struggle didn't stop!

Suddenly, Miles and the family burst in.

"Hey, hey, be careful, guys!" Mr. Stevens cautioned. "You don't want to break anything."

Ren arched an eyebrow at Louis. "Oh yes. I *do*," she replied.

Miles stepped up behind them. "Seriously," he warned, "the palace has deep spiritual meaning for the islanders."

"Does that mean it's *haunted*?" asked Donnie.

"No, on the contrary," Miles told him. "The islanders believe that the palace is a source of good fortune and positive energy."

37

"Blah, blah, blah," said Beans. "Where's the lady with the hugs?"

"Your island awaits you," Miles promised the Stevenses as he gestured to the lush vegetation and white-sand beaches beyond the tropical mansion's doors.

No one saw his wicked grin.

After changing into their beachwear, the Stevenses explored their island paradise.

Ren was scooped up and carried from the hot sand to the cool water by the smiling Mootai. Donnie went jogging along a jungle path—and found a trio of pretty young women in grass skirts following him.

"I can't believe this," he said with a grin. "I'm never going back!"

On the beach, Mr. and Mrs. Stevens sat blissfully under a palm frond. They wrapped their arms around each other while islanders fed them fruit.

Mrs. Stevens sighed happily. This sure beat doing Louis's laundry, she decided.

Meanwhile, as Donnie continued his jog, he

noticed a young man strolling by who looked very familiar.

"Oh, man," said the surprised Donnie. "You look just like this guy who used to go to my high school. . . . What was his name?"

"My name is Laylo," said the islander.

"No, no . . . Patrick Green!" said Donnie.

"My name is Laylo," said the young man. Then the smiling islander walked away.

"Are you sure, man?" Donnie asked, "because—"

"Hey, Donnie!" Louis called from the ocean waves. He was standing, perfectly balanced, on a surfboard. Of course, it helped that two islanders were *holding* the thing for him.

Even with the support, Louis flopped off the board and into the water. *Splash!*

Donnie kept jogging until he found his parents and Miles. "Hey, *guys!*" he called.

"Hey, Donnie," his father replied.

"Donnie! Having fun?" asked his mother.

"This place is the *best,*" Donnie said. "You want to hear something weird? I swear that one of the natives is this guy who went to my high school."

Mr. Stevens frowned. "Son, we're on an uncharted island. The last thing you're going to do is run into one of your classmates."

Then he and Miles laughed.

"Have a grape, son," suggested his mother. "They're delicious."

An islander popped a grape into Donnie's mouth. Shrugging, Donnie chewed.

Ren waded through the cool ocean water. She was trying *not* to think about Gil and how much he'd hurt her. But it wasn't easy.

Suddenly, Mootai waved and strode toward her. "Ren!" he called.

"Hey, Mootai!" Ren answered, giving him a smile.

"Can I serve you in any way?" he asked as he followed her along the shoreline.

"No," Ren assured him. "Everyone on the island has been great."

Mootai nodded. "So, you are having a pleasurable time on our island?"

"Yes," Ren said. "Completely."

Mootai looked unconvinced. "Yet in your eyes there is so much sadness."

"Yeah, I was just thinking about something," she admitted.

"Then you should think of something *else*," he advised. "Something *wonderful*."

Ren brightened a little. "Like what?"

"The smell of the ocean," Mootai suggested as he took a deep breath. Ren did the same. "The beauty of a flower . . ." Mootai stopped and handed her a beautiful red flower. She smiled. He added, "The light from your smile."

Ren blushed and laughed.

"You see?" he said. "The sadness is gone."

Just then, the hollow sound of the tribal conch shell echoed through the air.

"What was that?" asked Ren.

"Your family is being summoned for a great honor," Mootai explained.

The Stevens family arrived with their stomachs rumbling. It was dinnertime and they expected a big, delicious dinner. There were no restaurants or fast-food joints on the island, but in the lush tribal council area, the natives had their own specialty of the house: giant roasted worm on a stick.

"Come feast on this island delicacy," demanded Tuka.

Mr. Stevens forced a smile. "Thank you so much," he said, "for this delicious-looking . . . worm?"

"Actually, it's a slug," Miles said. "It's an island delicacy."

Each member of the Stevens family held one. The smiling islanders gathered and the family cringed.

"Are we really supposed to eat this?" Donnie asked with a look of disgust.

Miles sidled up to the Stevenses. "Uh, guys," he whispered, "the elders will be deeply offended if we refuse their offering."

The Stevens family looked up at their hosts. Tuka and the rest of the islanders gestured for them to eat and enjoy.

"I suppose it's the least we can do," Mr. Stevens said. He took a bite. The islanders smiled and murmured appreciatively. Mr. Stevens smiled back. He hated it. But he tried to be a good sport. "Yummm . . . that's good slug," he said. Then he gestured to his family to dig in.

Reluctantly, the family members nibbled on their toasted slugs. Only Beans chowed down like he'd been given a giant hot dog on the Fourth of July.

When Louis started to gag, Miles pulled him aside and asked, "Having trouble getting it down, huh?"

Louis nodded and admitted, "I, uh . . . generally try to avoid snacks that leave a trail of slime."

"Yeah, so does Tuka," Miles confided. "I happen to know for a fact that he has some American munchies hidden in the palace pantry."

"*Word?*" Louis whispered, his eyes wide.

"Word," Miles assured him.

Louis turned to the family. "Excuse me, I have to use the facilities," he announced. "Ren? Hold my slug." Louis handed it to Ren and rushed toward the house.

"Louis!" complained the vexed Ren.

"Where is he going?" Mrs. Stevens asked.

As the islanders grinned, urging them to eat, the family forced polite smiles on their faces and returned to their slug-fest.

Meanwhile, inside Tuka's palace, Louis checked every cabinet until he hit the one with the jackpot of snack food: popcorn, chips, candy, and more!

Louis filled his arms with goodies, then looked around for a place to eat. When he turned around, he noticed the door labeled FORBIDDEN CHAMBER OF MYSTERY: DO NOT OPEN!

"Forbidden Chamber of Mystery?" Louis murmured, intrigued. "Do not *open*? Yeah, right!"

His arms full of snack foods, Louis kicked at the door with his foot. It swung wide, revealing a beautiful room decorated with artifacts, masks, and headdresses.

At the end of the room sat a majestic throne. "Now *that's* a chair," Louis said in awe. This baby's almost as cool as my Lounge-O-Matic, he thought as he climbed onto the throne to relax.

"I know where *I'm* spending this vacation,"

Louis murmured as he popped open a bag of chips. He sat back and lazily munched—then he noticed a bamboo lever.

"Footrest lever, nice touch," he said as he pulled the lever back.

But the lever didn't make the throne recline. Instead, an ominous rumble sounded. Then, like a house of flimsy cards, the entire palace started to collapse!

Chapter 5

Louis squeezed his eyes shut in terror. The walls crumbled down. The roof flew away. And the regal palace became a royal junk heap.

When all was quiet again, Louis opened his eyes. He found himself still sitting on the throne—the rubble of the royal palace around him.

The horrified Stevens clan and all of the stunned islanders raced to the demolition scene. Louis meekly presented a token of apology to Tuka—

"C-c-c-corn snacky?" he offered.

"No!" roared Tuka, raising his arms over his head. "What have you done?!"

The islanders gathered around their furious chief. Fists were shaken. Oaths and threats were made.

The Stevens family huddled together. "Louis!" Mrs. Stevens cried. "What happened?"

"I thought it was a footrest," Louis sputtered. "I didn't know it was a house-collapser."

Miles rushed over and explained. "It appears your son sat in the forbidden throne, destroyed a sacred royal residence, and put a curse on the entire village."

"You don't really believe in all that, do you?" asked Mrs. Stevens.

"I don't," Miles said. "But they do." He gestured toward the wailing islanders.

"Good people of Mandelino," Mrs. Stevens announced as she grabbed Louis off the throne and pulled him behind her. "This was just an accident."

"Just an accident!" agreed the shaken Louis.

"Maybe there's some insurance policy for sacred dwellings or something," Mr. Stevens suggested hopefully.

"Listen, I think the less you say now, the better," Miles advised.

"Louis, how could you total our house?" asked Donnie.

"It totaled *itself*!" Louis screeched. "I swear that's what happened!"

Ren sighed in disgust. "Yeah, congratulations, Louis. You did it again," she said. "Anything that's nice or decent, you just end up ruining."

Louis grasped frantically at any straw he could think of. "At least now everyone has an ocean view!" he exclaimed.

A new chorus of angry complaints exploded from the family members.

"People! People!" Miles cried. The Stevens family quieted down, and Miles whispered, "Listen, I think the thing for you to do right now is get away from this area, pronto."

The islanders were still moaning and wailing at the destruction of their palace.

"What about our luggage?" whispered Mrs. Stevens.

"Well, officially it's cursed," Miles said. "So touching it would just make things worse."

Ren fumed. "And where are we supposed to live?"

Miles led them away from the village to a deserted stretch of beach. There the Stevens family cast forlorn stares at a pile of sticks, palm leaves, twine, and fish netting. Louis sat alone on a log.

"I guess you could put a lean-to together from this," Miles suggested.

"Lean-to?" Mr. Stevens asked. "We're *supposed* to be living in a palace!"

Miles backed away. "Obviously, that's no longer an option," he said. He paused for a moment. "Well, it's getting dark. You guys should get started."

"Wait a minute," said Beans. "Where are *you* sleeping?"

"Well, I have a small hut provided by the islanders," Miles said. "It only sleeps one . . .

comfortably. Don't worry, I'll check in on you later to see if you survived."

The Stevenses watched in mild shock as Miles left them on the open beach.

"*Survive?*" Mr. Stevens repeated uneasily. Then he bucked himself up. "Come on," he told his family. "Let's not panic. We've got a lot of work to do. Let's pitch in!"

Everyone picked up some materials. Ren drifted over to Louis and said, "You know, this *is* your fault."

"Ren, can we not talk about this? It was an accident. I'm sorry," Louis insisted.

"You shouldn't have even been in there, Louis," chided Ren.

"Well, Ren, I'm *sorry*," Louis repeated. "I'm not perfect, like you."

"I am *not* perfect," Ren argued.

"Really? Ren, let's look at this. You have perfect grades. You have perfect behavior. You have a perfect life."

"You don't know what's going on in my life!" she cried.

"So you had a little boyfriend trouble,

boo-hoo, Ren," Louis lectured. "Life goes on."

"You know what?" Ren cried as she stood up. "I do not want to talk about Gil. And if you were smart, you would shut your mouth."

"And what if I *wasn't* smart?" he threatened.

Mr. Stevens rushed over and separated them. "Hey, stop it, guys! We've got enough to deal with without you two being at each other's throats, okay?"

Mrs. Stevens joined the intervention. "You know what, Louis?" she said. "You and Donnie and I will go find some firewood. Ren, you and Beans will stay with Dad and help start the shelter."

"I'd rather eat," Beans said. "You got any more *slugs*?"

"Hey, Beans, we're all hungry," Donnie pointed out. "If we find some food, we'll pick it up and bring it back."

About an hour later, the sun began to set. Louis, Donnie, and Mrs. Stevens had gathered huge armfuls of firewood.

"Donnie . . . could you do me a favor?"

Louis begged, lagging behind. "Could you scratch my nose, please?"

He felt a hand reach out of the twilight jungle to scratch it.

"Thanks," Louis said. Then he screamed. The hand didn't belong to Donnie. It belonged to Miles. Louis ran over to where his mother and brother were standing.

"Good *news*, everyone!" Miles announced. "The council of elders is meeting right now. If you go before them and make a sincere, heartfelt apology, I am sure everything is going to be fine."

Mrs. Stevens breathed a sigh of relief. "Thank goodness! I'll go tell the others." She turned to leave.

"No, no, no! I'm sorry!" Miles said, grabbing her arm. "Mandelino tradition states that all apologies must be made in groups of three." He ushered them along toward the village. "Groups of three . . ."

Drums played in the village. Dancers whirled about and burning torches shone down on the rigid faces of the angry council elders.

Night had fully fallen as Louis, Mrs. Stevens, and Donnie were brought before a huge, carved Tiki head. Miles stood off to the side of the clearing. Tuka clapped his hands and the drumming and dancing ceased.

"Ooah! Let the boy speak!" cried Tuka.

"Go ahead, Donnie," said the petrified Louis. "You're stronger than I am!"

Donnie grabbed Louis by the collar of his shirt and pushed him toward the Tiki head. "Get over there!" he demanded.

"Okay, okay," Louis relented. He stood and addressed the council. "Good evening, ladies and gentlemen—"

"Speak to Fire God!" Tuka commanded.

Huh? Louis thought for a moment, then figured it out. "Oh, the big head," Louis said flatly.

The islanders all gasped.

"The big *sacred* head," Louis added. "Sacred head. Yeah, well, uh . . . I'm really sorry about the whole collapsing palace deal, and I promise I'll never destroy another palace again."

Tuka glared at Louis. "The God of Fire will

53

consider your apology. But first—we feast!" he declared.

A sumptuous dinner was laid out. Lobster, shrimp, and mountains of fresh fruit were heaped on platters. The villagers stared at Mrs. Stevens, Donnie, and Louis.

Mrs. Stevens looked at Miles. "It just doesn't seem right to eat without the rest of the family," she whispered.

"I understand," Miles assured her. "But it's your only chance for forgiveness."

Donnie and Louis practically drooled over the food. "See, Mom, we're not eating for ourselves," Donnie said. "We're eating for forgiveness."

Louis was already stuffing his face. "It's the right thing to do!" he assured them.

Meanwhile, down at the beach, the lean-to was almost finished. Mr. Stevens and Beans knelt inside and put the last touches on it.

"Could we order a pizza?" asked Beans.

"Put a lid on it, Beans," snapped Mr. Stevens. "We're *all* hungry."

54

Ren tossed another palm frond on top of the lean-to. "I'm gonna go see what's taking them so long," she said.

"Don't stray too far, honey," Mr. Stevens called.

Ren took off—and Beans threw Mr. Stevens a loopy grin. "Wanna go skinny-dipping?" he asked.

Mr. Stevens sighed. *This* is my dream vacation? he thought, and just shook his head.

Ren began to search diligently for the others. She followed the main path, brushing low-hanging branches out of her way as she moved.

Suddenly, she heard a *hiss*.

When she turned, she came face-to-face with a huge snake hanging from a tree.

She screamed!

Chapter 6

Mootai burst through the high bamboo. Leaping between Ren and the snake, Mootai hissed and grimaced while waving a flaming torch in his hand. Startled, the snake turned and slithered away.

"Thank you," Ren said, her heart thundering, her hands shaking. "That was *so* brave."

"Not so much," the handsome young man said calmly as he led her down the path. "You make face uglier than his. He runs away."

Ren smiled weakly.

"Now you are okay?" Mootai asked.

"No," Ren admitted. "My brother knocked our house down. I'm tired, I'm hungry, and . . ."

Mootai stopped walking and turned to look at Ren. "Please," he said as he took a string of shells from around his neck and held them out to her. "For you."

"What's this?" asked Ren warily.

"It is every shell you walked on when you first arrived on our island," he said as he placed them around her neck. "There."

Ren blushed and smiled at Mootai. He returned the smile. "From my heart," he said.

"Mootai, I'm not really ready for this. . . ." she said.

"Then I will wait," Mootai promised.

Ren's smile was pained. "How can everything be so horrible and so wonderful all at the same time?" she asked.

"Your troubles may soon be over," Mootai assured her. "Your mother and brothers are feasting with the elders right now."

"Feasting?" asked the surprised Ren.

"It is like eating, but with bigger plates," Mootai explained.

"I *know*," Ren said. "I thought they just went out there to get wood."

"Come, see with your eyes." Mootai took her by the hand and led her through the bamboo forest to the edge of the village.

As they approached a ring of torches, Ren heard laughing voices and tribal music. From the cover of night, Ren watched her mom and her two brothers chowing down like there was no tomorrow.

Shaking her head in disbelief, Ren asked, "How can they pig out like that when we're starving?"

"Your brother eats without chewing," Mootai observed.

Ren stared as Louis leaned over a tower of food and offered Donnie some fruit. She couldn't take any more of this.

"I'm going in," said Ren, and she headed for the festival table.

But when Miles saw her coming, he rushed to her and pulled her back into the shadows before her brothers and mother noticed. "Bad idea," he told her. "To interrupt a tribal feast would be unforgivable. Isn't that right, Mootai?"

"Unforgivable," Mootai nodded. "Yes."

"I don't understand," said Ren. "Why didn't they come and get us?"

"Well, I mentioned that to your family, and someone said, 'More for us,'" Miles replied.

"Now, who said *that*?" Ren crossed her arms in front of her chest. "Why am I asking?" she said with disgust. "It was Louis."

Then Ren turned and stormed back to the beach. Behind her, Donnie and Louis continued to dance—and eat—to the beat of the tribal drums.

When she reached the lean-to, Ren told her father what she'd seen. He listened while he tried again to make a fire.

"I mean, I could understand Louis selling us out," Ren said, "but Mom and Donnie? Why would they go along with him? It doesn't make sense!"

Engrossed in fire-making, her father simply grunted.

"Boy, you think you know a person," Beans said. He leaned over the smoking kindling. "Hey, it looks like you got a little action there, Smokey."

"No!" cried Mr. Stevens. "Step *away* from the fire!"

Putting a hand over Beans's face, Mr. Stevens held the boy back. The kid had already sneezed out his first fire. There was no way Mr. Stevens was going to let that happen again!

Back at the feast, Miles, Donnie, Mrs. Stevens, and Louis were relaxing. The tribal elders strode through the crowd and everyone stood to honor them.

Then Tuka and his council arrived at the giant Tiki head, and the drumming stopped. Tuka raised his staff to salute his goddess.

"Ohhhh Oprah!" he cried.

Confused, Mrs. Stevens turned to Miles. "Oprah?" she whispered.

"It's a coincidence," Miles assured her.

"Mighty Goddess of Fire, the Stevens family

has apologized," Tuka proclaimed. "They have feasted with us. Are they now worthy of forgiveness?"

Donnie and Louis raised their coconut cups in salute to the goddess. The Tiki head's eyes glowed red. The elders fell to their knees. Miles and the Stevenses dropped with them. A stream of fire burst from the Tiki head's mouth, the scorching plume reaching out over the heads of the kneeling revelers.

Louis whirled to face Miles. "Is that good?" he asked.

"Does it *look* good?" Miles replied.

Tuka nodded obedience to the goddess's decision. He approached the Stevens family, and then he performed a cutting motion with his hand.

"Well, they've made their decision," Miles said. "You're going to be shunned."

"Yes!" Donnie said excitedly.

"No, son," Mrs. Stevens said. "*Shunned* is bad."

Together the islanders turned their backs on the three Stevenses.

"You've been deemed unworthy of forgiveness," Miles explained. "No one on the island can have anything to do with you."

"Well, why don't they tell us to our faces?" Donnie asked as he stood. Louis, Mrs. Stevens, and Miles also rose.

"Because then they'd have to kill you," said Miles.

"Right, well," Donnie squeaked. "Unworthy's good for me."

"Yeah, it's good," agreed Louis uneasily.

Mrs. Stevens shook her head. "Miles, I want my family out of here on the next plane," she firmly demanded.

"Absolutely," Miles agreed. "Seven days from now, you'll all be heading home."

Mrs. Stevens couldn't believe it. "Seven *days*?" she squeaked.

"That's the next plane," Miles said.

Mr. Stevens's fire was blazing nicely by the time Louis, Donnie, and Mrs. Stevens got back to the beach.

"Look, honey!" Mrs. Stevens exclaimed,

rushing up to her husband. "You built a shelter *and* you made a fire!"

"They smell like *pork*," Beans said as he sniffed Mrs. Stevens's shirt.

"So," Ren said as she strolled in between her brothers. "How was your *feast*?"

Louis smiled nervously. "What feast?" he asked.

"Don't give me that. I saw with my own eyes," Ren told him. "And it wasn't pretty. You have a little something on your cheek."

Ren joined her father and Beans on the other side of the fire from the well-fed feasters, as Louis touched the piece of pineapple on his face.

"Okay, okay," Mrs. Stevens said apologetically. "I wanted to bring everyone, but they said there was a rule about groups of three."

"Really?" Mr. Stevens asked skeptically. "How convenient."

Donnie waved his hands. "Hey, Dad, we only ate all the food so we could be forgiven by Oprah," he tried to explain.

"I see," said Mr. Stevens. "And did Oprah forgive us?"

Louis shrugged. "Almost. There's a little thing about being shunned. . . ."

"I know it sounds great, but it's not," Donnie said.

"So we did all the work, and they get all the food?" Beans cried. *"That* seems fair."

Mrs. Stevens couldn't believe she was hearing this. "You think we would sell you out for a dinner?" she charged.

"And flaming dessert," Louis added.

Mrs. Stevens smacked Louis with her sun hat. "Quiet, Louis." She spun back to face her husband. "I find this completely insulting."

"Insulting," Mr. Stevens repeated, annoyed. "You weren't even going to *tell* us about it!"

"Because I didn't want you to feel bad. You know, my group ate, yours didn't," explained Mrs. Stevens.

Mr. Stevens turned red with anger. "Why would I feel *bad*? I've provided *plenty* of food for this family over the years," he declared.

"Steve, who said you haven't?" Mrs. Stevens interjected quickly. She realized she'd touched on a sore subject.

Suddenly, Louis let out a huge burp. Mrs. Stevens turned around and glared at her son. Then everyone jumped when a clap of thunder boomed and water poured down on them.

"Great," snapped Ren. "Just what we need. It's raining!"

"At least I was able to put a roof over our heads," Mr. Stevens said huffily.

They all ran under the protection of the lean-to, which turned out to be meager shelter against the storm. At least it got them together. . . .

Glaring. Angry. Accusing.

But together.

Chapter 7

In a grassy clearing on the other side of the island, a small camp had been set up. Modern trailers and huge canvas tents sheltered an array of television equipment and dressing rooms for actors.

In the biggest tent, a large TV screen showed a video of the Stevens family huddling in their lean-to against the storm.

The TV screen then switched to several scenes of the family's first day on the island: their arrival, their fun on the beach, their slug-fest, and finally, the destruction of the Royal

Palace. Suddenly, a graphic appeared across the screen: FAMILY FAKE-OUT!

Miles stood before a bank of monitors while a makeup artist dabbed at his face.

"Okay, Miles," urged the director, Keith. "On-air commentary in five, four, three, two . . ."

Miles strolled over to the camera. "Quite a first day for our unsuspecting vacationers," he said into the camera. A TV screen next to Miles showed a tightly edited tape of highlights.

"They still have no idea they're on TV," explained Miles, "that all the natives are actors, and that everything that's happening to them is completely controlled by our crew. Luckily, we know a lot more about them than they know about us. Thanks to a little help from their friends. . . ."

Back in Sacramento, Tawny Dean and Alan Twitty sat, horrified, watching the show in Tawny's family room.

"I think I made a terrible mistake," Twitty said.

Tawny was stunned. "I can't believe you set them up for this!" she cried.

On TV, Miles grinned and continued, "Our

secret source tipped us off that Louis, the irrepressible little brother, could never resist a 'keep out' sign, let alone a comfortable chair."

The sign for the forbidden chamber was displayed on the screen. Then, Louis plopped down on the throne.

"You told them that?" Tawny asked Twitty. "What else did you tell them?"

Twitty's brow knitted with guilt. "Everything," he confessed.

"Oh, nice work," Tawny told him.

"I thought it'd be *fun*," he said.

Tawny gestured at the television. "Does it look like they're having fun?" she demanded.

Twitty shook his head. On the screen, Louis and Beans huddled together.

"Beans, hold me," said the shivering Louis.

Back in the production compound, Miles snickered. "Let's pump up the rain a little, fellas," he told his director. "Cue thunder."

"Cue thunder!" repeated Keith. A technician turned a dial. On the monitor, the sound of thunder seemed to shake the sky.

"I want to go home!" Ren cried.

Miles smiled, "I'm sure you do. But we have a few more surprises in store for you. Tune in every day to see if the Stevens family can survive a week in 'paradise.'"

Unbeknownst to Ren, her best friends from school were watching her that very minute.

In Ruby's bedroom, Ruby and Monique shook their heads.

"Poor Ren," moaned Monique. "How humiliating."

"Well . . . maybe nobody's watching," suggested Ruby hopefully.

But *everyone* was watching. Even at the Roller Cakes diner, every last customer was glued to *Family Fake-Out!*

Finally, Miles wrapped up. "From this summer's most outrageous new reality show, *Family Fake-Out!*, I'm your host, Miles McDermott, saying, 'Isn't life funny . . . when it's not happening to you?' Good night!"

Larry Beale clapped from his seat at the Roller Cakes counter. "Yes!" Larry burst out. "Brilliant! I love it!"

No one reacted to Larry. "Come on, guys," Larry cried to the restaurant, "they're *miserable*. It's hilarious. Come on!"

At the TV show's base camp, huge tents lined the area, and there were trailers for costumes, props, makeup, and more.

Miles rushed across the compound, closely trailed by a couple of young, overeager assistants named Scott and Brooke.

"*Great* show, Miles," Scott said enthusiastically.

"*Excellent* show," agreed Brooke.

"Better than *Gotcha!*?" asked Miles.

"No doubt," Brooke answered instantly.

Scott hopped into the driver's seat of a golf cart. "*Family Fake-Out!* is the best reality show on TV!"

"Are you just saying that because your jobs depend on it?" Miles asked as he slid into the passenger seat.

"No, of *course* not," Scott weaseled.

"You're ten times better a host than that Lance Lebow," Brooke added as she climbed into the back.

Miles glared ahead as they sped through the camp. Just the mention of Lance's name was enough to make his blood boil.

"You know," Miles told them, not for the first time, "when I was the producer of *Gotcha!*, I hired Lance Lebow. And how did he repay me?"

"He got you *fired*," Scott replied as he braked the golf cart before Miles's trailer.

"That *ingrate*," Brooke hissed, desperate to show Miles her undying loyalty.

Miles climbed from the golf cart and headed for his trailer. He stopped at the door.

"Don't worry, Miles," Scott said as he chased after his boss. "When the ratings come out, you'll be on top."

"I'd *better*," warned Miles, "or heads are gonna roll!" Miles raised a single eyebrow as he threw his toadies a threatening look. "Now, what do we have for tomorrow?"

Brooke offered a folder to Miles. The host snatched it and was about to enter his trailer when he heard a technician call out, "Hey, Patrick! Close call!"

Miles spun around in time to see "Laylo" step out of another trailer in street clothes.

"Patrick Green!" Miles grinned as he dismissed his toadies and walked over to the actor. "We need to *talk*."

"Look, I'm sorry that Donnie recognized me," Patrick said. "I graduated three years ago. I can't believe the kid still remembers me. But from now on, I'll keep a low profile, that's what I'll do."

Miles's gaze was icy. "Here's a better idea," he said. "You're *fired*." Miles turned sharply and stormed back to his trailer—leaving Patrick standing there in stunned disappointment.

"Wait," said Miles suddenly turning back to the forlorn actor. "I just thought of something," he said. "According to our research, Donnie's not exactly the Einstein of the family. We can have some fun with this. You're rehired."

Pleased with himself, Miles sauntered toward his trailer. He didn't get far before a technician grabbed him and anxiously thrust a mechanical squirrel at him.

"What do you think, Miles?" the technician

asked. Cute as a button, the squirrel wiggled its nose.

"It's adorable," said Miles. "Fix it. I *hate* adorable."

"Fix it," muttered the technician as "Lord and Master" Miles walked off with his chin in the air.

The next morning, the *Family Fake-Out!* theme song began to play once again on TV screens all over the country.

"Now it's time for America's favorite new reality show," a chipper voice announced. "*Family Fake-Out!* With your host, Miles McDermott!"

Inside the command tent, Miles strode toward the camera.

"Hi, that's me!" he said, smiling into the lens. "I'm Miles McDermott. Welcome to *Family Fake-Out!* Thank you for joining us for our morning edition. The Stevens family is just waking up. Yesterday we knocked down their house, deprived them of modern conveniences, and gave them a good soaking to boot! . . . Let's see how far we can push this family today—" Miles grinned widely—"before they *crack.*"

The Stevens family woke up cold, dirty, hungry, and still wearing clothes from the day before.

"All right, Mrs. Stevens," commanded Mr. Stevens. "This time, you and the boys take care of the fire. I'll take Ren and Beans and find us some food."

"Good luck," Mrs. Stevens told him.

"I don't need *luck* to find food for my family," Mr. Stevens barked defensively.

"Okay," she said, backing off. Then she worriedly watched the "proud hunters" head into the jungle.

Back in TV land, Miles laughed, watching the screen. Mr. Stevens stormed away from camp with Ren and Beans in tow.

"Looks like Steve's a little sensitive this morning," Miles said with a chuckle. "According to our research, he's been out of work for quite a while. Maybe the fact that *Mrs.* Stevens has been bringing home the bacon is finally starting to get to him." Miles smiled mischievously. "I'll see if I can *help*."

* * *

Mr. Stevens, Ren, and Beans hiked through the jungle, the cries of animals echoing around them.

Mr. Stevens signaled the group to stop, then motioned for them to kneel. Near the ground they spied a cute little squirrel hopping onto a log.

"Oh, Daddy," whispered Ren, "we're not gonna kill that cute little squirrel, are we?"

"That's not cute, that's *breakfast*," Mr. Stevens replied. He advanced on the squirrel. Just as he was about to grab it, the squirrel suddenly jumped onto its hind legs and growled ferociously!

Oh, no, thought Mr. Stevens. *Rabid squirrel!*

Then all three of the "proud hunters" were off and running, the crazed squirrel chasing them through the jungle. In seconds, the screaming trio plowed straight into Miles!

"Miles!" Mr. Stevens said breathlessly. He looked around. The manic squirrel had suddenly vanished.

"Something wrong?" Miles asked.

"Okay. We're tired, we're hungry!" shrieked Ren. "And we just got attacked by a killer squirrel!"

"Don't worry, guys," Miles said quickly. "I've arranged for an emergency food drop. That should get you through the week."

"Oh! Thanks, Miles!" Mr. Stevens said, relieved.

Miles glanced up as a plane's engine revved overhead. "There it is now!" he told them.

Casting their gazes to the sky, Mr. Stevens, Ren, and Beans spotted the plane and waved their arms.

"Hey!" yelled Mr. Stevens. "Hey! Hey! We're over here! We're over *here*!"

A huge wooden crate on a parachute dropped from the plane. But instead of falling toward the beach, it plunged onto a mountaintop.

"No!" Mr. Stevens screamed.

"I'm sorry," Miles said, clucking his tongue. "The wind must have blown it off course."

Beans licked his finger and held it up. "The wind's blowing the *other* way," he said.

Ren eyed Miles suspiciously.

76

"Quite the little weather man you've got there," Miles said with a nervous laugh. "Looks like you folks have some mountain climbing to do."

Mr. Stevens frowned. "Miles, this isn't exactly familiar territory," he pointed out.

"I would ask the islanders to help you guys," Miles said uncomfortably, "but whenever I mention your names, they shake with anger."

Mr. Stevens worriedly eyed the mountain.

"Come on, you guys can do it," Miles said. "Just follow these red trail markers."

Mr. Stevens frowned. "All right. But I should let Mrs. Stevens know."

"Come on, Steve," challenged Miles. "Do you really need your *wife's* help to bring home the bacon?"

That did it! Mr. Stevens reddened. "Okay, let's go, people!" he cried, puffed up with fatherly pride. "We've got a family to feed!"

Miles watched the trio hit the mountain trail. Then he grinned with glee—because the worse things looked for the Stevens family, the better things looked for him!

77

Chapter 8

In the *Family Fake-Out!* control tent, Keith, the director, glanced at a line of TV screens and noticed that Donnie was gathering firewood on one of them.

"Donnie's alone," Keith said into a microphone. "Cue Laylo!"

Donnie fumbled with the huge mound of broken branches in his arms.

"Hey, Donnie!" called a familiar voice. Donnie was stunned as Laylo strolled over—

sporting a high school sweater and carrying schoolbooks! Donnie's eyes widened. Was he going *nuts*?

"What are you staring at, man?" Laylo asked. "You know, you're gonna be late for class."

Donnie did a double take. "You *are* Patrick Green!" he cried. "What are you doing here?"

"Don't tell anyone. I'm cutting English." Laughing, "Laylo" ran away.

"Dude . . . !" Donnie was about to go after Patrick when a hidden cameraman pulled a wire and tripped him. He slammed down heavily, and by the time he got up again, Patrick was gone.

Donnie raced back to the beach to tell Louis and his mother. "Guys," he cried, "that native who looked like Patrick Green. He *was* Patrick Green!"

"What are you talking about?" asked Louis.

"I just saw him," Donnie shouted.

Mrs. Stevens took the firewood from her son. "Now, honey . . . just because someone slightly resembles someone else—"

"He was wearing the school sweater," Donnie said urgently. "He was cutting English!"

Mrs. Stevens sighed. "Donnie, this is ridiculous," she said.

"Why is *everything* that I do in this family so ridiculous?" demanded Donnie. "If anyone else said it, you'd believe them."

"Honey, you're hungry," Mrs. Stevens cooed. "You've been in the sun."

"Donnie, relax," advised Louis. "This morning I thought I saw a cheeseburger doing yoga."

Donnie glared at his brother. "I know what I saw," he said.

Miles approached. "Hey, folks," he called.

Mrs. Stevens rushed up to him. "Miles, I heard a plane before!" she cried angrily. "You told me there's not going to be another plane here for a week."

"It didn't land," Miles said sadly. "I arranged a food drop for you, but it missed the beach and landed on the mountain." He pointed the way.

"Whatever. Can't you just sneak us a meal or something?" Louis asked.

Miles raised his voice. "Don't you realize I'm risking everything just by *talking* to you?"

"How do we get the food?" asked Donnie.

"Go to the big rock on the beach, head into the woods, and then follow the blue trail markers."

"I think we should wait for Dad and the others," Donnie suggested.

"No, actually, they already went up there," Miles said.

"Without telling us?" howled Mrs. Stevens.

"They did mention something about you guys having had enough food last night," Miles lied.

"Oh, okay, I get it," said Louis. "It's payback."

Miles shrugged. Louis fumed, "I tell you, you have *one* little feast and it's all up in flames!" Louis threw down his shirt and ran off toward the trail. The others rushed to follow him.

Miles snatched up Louis's shirt and grinned at the closest hidden camera. "This'll come in handy."

When Louis, Mrs. Stevens, and Donnie reached the top of the mountain trail, they found a crate and a parachute.

"Food!" cried Louis.

They rushed over to the clearing. The crate

was open, but empty. Crushed food boxes were strewn all over.

"They got here first and ate everything," Donnie said dejectedly.

"I hate payback," Louis muttered.

Mrs. Stevens fumed. She threw a couple of empty boxes into the air. "Now it's on!" she cried.

Meanwhile, at the end of *another* mountain trail, Ren, Mr. Stevens, and Beans stepped into a clearing. They spied a crate and a parachute.

"There it is!" Mr. Stevens hollered. "Food!"

The three hungry vacationers searched through the boxes, but there was nothing left to eat. Mr. Stevens was furious. "It's empty!" he cried.

"Who ate it all?" Beans bellowed.

Ren found Louis's shirt on the crate and waved it at her father and Beans. "Oh, yeah?" she said. "One guess!"

"Come on," said Mr. Stevens as he led his hungry group back down the mountain trail.

Hidden in the nearby bushes, a grinning cameraman taped their every move.

Back in the control tent, Miles smiled at the camera.

"Two trails. Two empty crates. And two hungry teams each thinking the other betrayed them. You gotta love it."

But did the audience? Back in Sacramento, the viewers weighed in.

"I think it's disgraceful," said Principal Wexler, as he watched the program from his recliner.

At Roller Cakes, Twitty and Tawny were also witnessing the trials and tribulations of the Stevens family.

"I hate this. I can't believe I sold them out," Twitty said, as he poured tons of syrup on his pancakes.

Tawny gaped. "Twitty," she said, "you can't drown your guilt in syrup."

"You're right," Twitty said with a sigh. Then he grabbed a canister and tried to *smother* his guilt with whipped cream.

Coach Tugnut walked up and nodded at the TV on the wall. "Hey," he said, "is this the greatest show of all time or what?" He noticed Twitty's whipped-cream covered, syrup-soaked pancakes. "Ooh, Twitty. You gonna finish those?"

"Yeah," Twitty said.

Tugnut looked crestfallen. "Anyway," he continued, "it's nice to see that for once, the joke's on Louis Stevens. Too bad the whole family has to go down with him."

Twitty sighed, feeling even more guilty.

"Twitty, you look like you're full. I'll finish those for you. Come on, bring 'em on," Tugnut urged.

"Take 'em," Twitty said, sliding the plate over.

The coach chowed down. His mouth full, Tugnut garbled, "And the best part is, those lunkheads *think* they're halfway around the world!"

"What did you say?" Twitty asked.

Tugnut swallowed. "I said—they think they're halfway around the world."

"Where are they?" Twitty asked urgently.

"Catalona," Tugnut told him. "Just a couple of miles off the coast. They flew around in circles for hours to fool 'em."

Tawny gaped at him, openmouthed. "How do you know that?" she demanded.

Tugnut informed them, "Oh, I went on one of these things called a *Web site*. They've got all the inside stuff."

Twitty and Tawny raced toward the door. "Catalona," Tawny said excitedly. "We're so close!"

Twitty nodded. "If we could just get out there, we could tell them what's going on."

Tawny thought about it. "All we really need is a boat, right?"

Tawny and Twitty knew exactly where they could get a boat. They took a bus to a dock by the ocean. There they found their friend Tom swabbing the deck of the SS *Doris*, his beloved sailboat.

"Ahoy, mateys!" Tom called when he saw Tawny and Twitty. "What brings you landlubbers down to the salty brine?"

Twitty narrowed his eyes at Tom's *Gilligan's Island* getup—a blue blazer, white bell-bottoms, and a yachting cap. "Speak English, please," Twitty demanded.

"Oh, excuse me," Tom apologized. "Whazzup?"

"Tom," Tawny quickly broke in, "have you been watching *Family Fake-Out!*?"

"I have," Tom said. "And I must say that I'm appalled as a sailor and a human being to see a family we know and love being tortured like that. Although, I did love that frisky squirrel!"

Tawny had to laugh with him. "Yeah, me too," she admitted.

"Well, um . . . it's all our fault," Twitty revealed. He caught Tawny's disapproving glare, then added, "All *my* fault. I set them up."

Tom frowned. "I'm doubly appalled," he said.

"You can help us, Tom," offered Tawny. "And you could help Louis."

"Well, Louis is my friend . . . when it suits him," he added. "And I can accept that. What can I do?"

"Can you sail this tub to Catalona?" Twitty asked.

"Welcome aboard," said Tom. Tawny and Twitty grinned. Soon they were off to rescue their friends!

Chapter 9

On the island, the production crew was in overdrive.

"Welcome to *Family Fake-Out!—Prime Time!*" Miles exclaimed into the camera. "This afternoon we wanted to see how far we could push our family until they finally cracked. For the answer, let's take a look at what our hidden cameras saw."

On the nearby television screen, the two warring factions of the Stevens clan clashed on the beach.

Donnie demanded, "How could you steal all our food?"

Ren snarled. "As *usual*, Donnie, you have *everything* backward."

"Are you calling me stupid?" Donnie shouted.

"No," Ren snapped. "I am calling you a *liar*."

Now it was Louis's turn. "You guys had to get back at us, huh? Thank you."

"But we got the evidence," Beans barked as he held out Louis's shirt and shook it before his pal. "How do you explain this, Louis?"

"You stole my food *and* my shirt?" Louis screeched. Louis snatched the shirt from Beans. "Give me that, you gassy little worm eater!"

"Don't talk to him like that!" warned Ren.

Louis laughed. "Oh, what? Is Beans your little boyfriend now?"

"You do *not* have a right to talk!" Ren pointed an accusing finger. "*You* cause all the trouble and *you* eat all the food!"

"Okay, enough!" Mrs. Stevens broke in. "Enough, kids. Stop! You kids shouldn't fight just because your father's trying to teach *me* a lesson."

Mr. Stevens recoiled. "And what would *that* be?" he demanded.

Mrs. Stevens faced her husband. "Look, Steve, I know that you are upset that you have been out of work and you are trying to show Ren and Beans that you can put food in their mouths."

"*What?*" cried Steve.

"But you could have left a little something for us." Mrs. Stevens said with a barely restrained sniffle.

"Don't twist this around," Mr. Stevens snarled. "There wasn't a crumb of food left when we got up there. It's almost like you're trying to *make* me look bad."

"Now you are losing it," Mrs. Stevens said.

Naturally, Mr. Stevens lost it. "Don't tell me I'm losing it!" he bellowed.

"Don't you yell at me in front of my family!" Mrs. Stevens shrieked.

"It's my family, too!" Mr. Stevens pointed out.

"Hold on, hold on!" Louis intervened. "Mom, we don't need them. We'll be fine on our own, thank you."

"Oh, really?" said Ren. "Well, *you* can sleep out in the rain tonight."

"We *can*," Louis screeched, "and we *will*!"

Shoving Louis away, Ren spun around and stormed off. Snapping "ha!" and "fine!" at each other, the two groups went their separate ways.

Inside the TV show's control tent, Miles's expression turned fiendish.

"Looks like things are getting personal," he told the camera. "And *interesting*. Speaking of which, let's catch up with our hot young couple, Ren and Mootai. Ren, known back home for her boyfriend troubles, is having a little better luck here on the island. . . ."

Ren was gazing sadly at a majestic waterfall when Mootai stepped into view. He sat before her on a large flat rock.

"Ren . . ." Mootai murmured soulfully.

Ren leaned in close. "Mootai . . ."

"The elders have forbidden me to see you," Mootai told her. They gazed into each other's eyes.

"Then you should leave," she told him softly.

"I can't," he said.

"Why not?" Ren's fingertips tingled as he took her hand.

"Because no matter what they would do to me, to be away from you would be worse," Mootai told her.

"Mootai . . ." Ren shook her head. "Everything is falling apart. You're the only good thing that's happened to me since I've been on this island."

Ren thought about the way Gil had hurt her. It was so hard to trust another boy. And yet . . .

"I would very much like to kiss you now," Mootai said gently.

In the control tent, Miles grinned at the screen.

"What do *you* think?" he told the camera. "Will Ren let Mootai kiss her? Vote now on familyfake-out.com!"

Across the nation, viewers responded instantly. In Ruby's bedroom, she and Monique were glued to the screen—and coming *unglued* at the same time!

"Don't do it!" warned Monique. "He's an *actor*."

"But he's so *cute*," Ruby said as she typed furiously on her laptop—which was logged onto the show's Web site. "Yes, yes, yes!" Ruby voted.

Across town, the horrified Principal Wexler banged the keys of his own computer. "No, no, no!" he shouted.

On the screen, Ren and Mootai gazed into each other's eyes as a question was printed below them: WILL REN LET MOOTAI KISS HER? The insta-poll numbers registered quickly—in favor of the kiss!

Ren's face drifted close to Mootai's. "I would, uh . . . very much like to kiss you, too," she said. Her lips parted for the kiss, holding the nation spellbound. Then Ren pulled back. "But I'm just not ready. I'm so sorry."

In the control tent, Miles turned from his monitor in astonishment. "Whoa, there's a surprise! But the week is still young. Our family may be splitting up, but Ren and Mootai are definitely *heating* up!"

* * *

Later that day, at the heart of the production company's base camp, a trailer door opened and "Mootai" emerged.

The bronzed actor met with a crowd of enthusiastic extras.

"Hey, Jason, way to go, man!" one actor cried.

"All right!" another yelled.

Jason/Mootai smiled. "Thanks," he said and shook a dozen hands. He met up with Miles and together they walked through the back lot.

"Nice scene today, kid," said Miles.

Jason smiled. "Thanks, Miles."

"Almost looked like you *liked* her," Miles fished.

"Well, I do," Jason admitted. "I mean—my *character*, Mootai, likes her."

Just then, Brooke and Scott rushed up with an urgent fax.

"Miles, the ratings are in!" Brooke exclaimed.

Miles nodded. "All right. Let me hear it."

Scott beamed. "We beat *Gotcha!* by one point!" He and Brooke high-fived each other.

"Beautiful," said Miles. Then his smile fell.

"But not quite satisfying enough. I want to *bury* them."

Brooke and Scott blanched. Miles turned to Jason. "Tomorrow you gotta get that kiss," he commanded.

"I think it can happen," said Jason.

"And after you kiss her," said Miles, "*dump* her."

Then Miles and his toadies hurried off, leaving Jason with a knot in the pit of his stomach—and a big decision to make.

Meanwhile, as the sun set over the ocean, a bright yellow life raft bobbed through the rough surf. Inside, Tawny and Twitty rowed furiously toward the beach.

Tom's sailboat had taken them all the way from Sacramento to Catalona Island. But the waves near the shore were so rough, Tom refused to sail them all the way in. Instead, he put them in his inflatable dinghy.

"Okay, we're almost there," Twitty said, still rowing. "I think that's the worst—"

Behind them, a towering wave rose from the

surf—and crashed down over the dinghy! Twitty went overboard, but his life jacket saved him.

"Twitty!" cried Tawny.

"I'm okay," Twitty hollered. "I can swim from here. I'll meet you on shore."

Nodding, Tawny rowed into shore. She soon stepped out of the boat and wandered onto the moonlit tropical paradise.

"Alan! Twitty!" called Tawny as she scouted around. "Alan! Where are you?"

Exhausted, she stumbled to a palm tree and paused to rest. She never even saw the plummeting coconut that knocked her out cold.

Some time later, Twitty dragged himself out of the water and across the sand. He was shouting Tawny's name when two burly security guys rushed in and grabbed him, dragging him away.

He was hauled kicking and screaming to the television show's base camp. They plopped him down on a carved throne with a fake stone Tiki head. Then they started questioning him.

"Okay, I'll tell you again," said Twitty for the

tenth time in a row. "I've never *met* the Stevens family. My name is Lars Honeytoast. I'm a marine biologist and I'm here on top-secret government business. So, if you'll just let me go—"

Twitty moved to leave—and the guards shoved him back on the throne. Miles, who had been walking by them, froze at the sound of the young captive's voice.

"Wait a minute," Miles said, stopping and looking. "You're that Twitty kid who turned us on to the Stevens family."

Twitty aimed an accusing finger in the producer's direction and said, "You *lied* to me, man. You said the show is fun, and it's not. It's cruel." Twitty tried to make his eyes hard and defiant. He managed. Kind of. "So, all that stuff I told you about? You can't use it anymore."

Miles shrugged. "I see," he said calmly. Then he beckoned to the guard. "Crate him!"

The guards grabbed Twitty and dragged him to a wardrobe trailer. They tossed him in and locked the door. Twitty kicked it, but it wouldn't budge. He turned away and sighed. That's when he realized rows of islander costumes were hanging all around him.

He snatched one up, a plan already taking shape in his mind.

Chapter 10

It was a new day on the island—and that meant brand-new opportunities for mastermind Miles McDermott.

"Welcome to *Family Fake-Out!*" Miles announced to his TV viewers. "When we left the Stevenses, they were split into two angry factions." He grinned. "I have a feeling that today things can only get worse. . . ."

At the base of a towering tree, Donnie, Louis, and Mrs. Stevens climbed out from under a pile of palm fronds. They were stiff, dirty, miserable—and their clothes were now tattered and shredded.

Louis shrugged. "That wasn't so bad, huh?"

"We slept on *dirt*!" protested Mrs. Stevens.

"Yeah," agreed Louis. "So, what's for breakfast?"

"The same as yesterday," said Donnie. "A big skillet full of nothing."

"Stop being so negative," said Louis. Then he stopped and checked his pockets. "Wait a second. . . ." With a flourish, he whipped a single peanut from his pocket. Donnie drooled. Mrs. Stevens's eyes widened.

"A peanut!" Donnie said excitedly. He and his mom closed in on Louis.

"Let's divide it—" said Donnie.

"Hold on, hold on!" Louis cried. Mrs. Stevens took out a nail file. Louis handed her the peanut and she commenced with the delicate operation.

"Careful, Ma!" cautioned Donnie.

"I know," said Mrs. Stevens, concentrating hard.

"Could I have the little stubby tail?" Louis mewled.

"You will *get* what she *gives* you!" roared Donnie.

"It's my peanut!" Louis yelled defensively. "And you don't even like the tail."

"Stop it!" Mrs. Stevens rose up between her warring sons. "We will each get a third and then we'll save the little stubby tail for dessert."

"Fine, whatever," cried Donnie. "Let's just eat it!"

Mrs. Stevens carefully went back to sawing their treasure into equal shares—and shuddered as it popped from her fingers.

Suddenly, a passing squirrel snatched it up!

"You bucktoothed, breakfast-nabbing little . . ." Louis muttered springing at the creature. "I want my peanut!"

The squirrel skittered away, but Louis was hot on the trail of the fuzzy little thief!

On the beach, the disheveled and dirty Ren woke with a shiver. She peered around and was surprised to see that the fire was out—and the timbers were soggy. But it hadn't rained!

Ren woke her father, but he couldn't figure out why the fire was out, either. He'd been stoking it all night.

"Beans, do you know what happened to this fire?" asked Mr. Stevens.

Bean furrowed his brow. "Let's see. I woke up to go to the bathroom," he said. "Oh, yeah!"

Ren shuddered. "Oh, that is gross."

"I hope you're satisfied," Mr. Stevens told Ren.

"What did I do?" cried Ren.

"*You* brought the kid along!" Mr. Stevens snarled.

"On a lousy vacation that you forced us to go on!" Ren countered.

"Hold on," Mr. Stevens shouted, "you couldn't *wait* to get out of town after what's his name broke up with you!"

Shocked and hurt, Ren glared at her father.

Suddenly, his expression softened. "Ren, I'm sorry," he said.

"I *hate* this family!" Ren wailed. She turned and sprinted down the shoreline.

Farther down the beach, Mootai sat on a rock staring out at the ocean. Ren ran for him as if he were her salvation. "Mootai . . ." she called.

"Ren," he said with concern as she approached.

"I want to go home," she said, tears threatening to fall. They gazed into each other's eyes—and then Ren flung herself into his arms.

Mootai held her. "All I can say is, one day very soon you will be home with your family and it will seem as though *none* of this was real," he told her.

Uh-oh, thought Miles, rushing into the control tent. He stared worriedly at the feed from the "Lovers' Cam."

"What's he saying?" Miles asked his assistant.

"I don't know," came the answer.

"No," Ren murmured on the TV screen. "The only thing that I want to be real is you."

"Okay, that's better," Miles said with a sigh of relief. "That's better. . . ."

Holding tight to Mootai, Ren said softly, "I wish that we were the only ones on this island . . . that nothing else existed." She drew back from their embrace and looked into his eyes.

"That is how I feel when I'm with you," Mootai said, holding her with his gaze.

"The other day, it's not that I didn't want to kiss you," Ren admitted. "I don't want to get hurt again."

Mootai caressed the side of her face. "I do not want to hurt you."

Ren felt it in her heart. "I believe you," she said.

Across the country, viewers were glued to their sets. Monique and Ruby were wide-eyed. And in Roller Cakes, even the scowling Larry gaped at the screen as Ren's lips gently met Mootai's in a long kiss.

A great sigh rose up from the Roller Cakes customers. Larry walked away. "You bunch of saps!" he complained.

At the end of the counter, Coach Tugnut

downed his pancakes and wept. "Their love is so *pure!*" he sobbed.

Back in Ruby's bedroom, Ruby said, "That is so beautiful."

Monique shook her head. "Gee, maybe you forgot. . . . It's not *real!*"

"Who cares?" said Ruby. "It's so romantic!"

On the beach, Ren and Mootai's kiss felt as if it might go on forever. But it didn't. Mootai pulled away.

"I can't . . ." he said dropping his island accent. "I can't do this."

"What—what's wrong?" gasped Ren.

"I'm supposed to break up with you!" he told her.

In the control tent, Miles watched the monitor in horror. "I was afraid of this," he growled grimly as he burst into action.

"Code red! Code red!" he cried. "Get Tuka in there and get Mootai *out.*"

Jason, the actor playing Mootai, scanned the

beach anxiously. "Look . . . look, you need to know . . ." he began, but he didn't get any further.

Tuka and three big islanders plowed out of the jungle and rushed toward him. "Mootai!" Tuka cried fiercely. "Mootai, this is forbidden!"

The trio of islanders—all built like linebackers—grabbed Mootai/Jason and hauled him away while Tuka ran interference. "Ren—!" Mootai/Jason cried.

"Get him out of here now!" Tuka commanded.

The tribal leader waved his hands and blocked Ren, preventing her from chasing after her man.

"Why are you *doing* this?" Ren called. "Mootai!"

She fixed her angry gaze on Tuka. "Why can't you just leave us *alone*?"

Back in the control tent, Miles snatched the mike from his director.

"Blame it on her brother Louis!" he instructed Tuka.

Tuka shuffled before Ren and cried, "This is all Louis's fault. Yes. . . . Yes!"

"*What*?" Ren roared. "What does *he* have to do with this?"

Tuka desperately tapped at the hidden receiver in his ear. "Uh-uh" he stammered. "That is a good question."

"Just say Louis told you they were meeting," Miles whispered through Tuka's earpiece. "He's to blame for everything."

"Your brother told us about your secret meetings with Mootai," Tuka told her. "He is to blame for all your unhappiness. Louis!"

Seething, Ren coldly hissed, "*Louis*."

Blinded by a crimson haze of rage, Ren bolted in search of her brother.

Chapter 11

A glorious feast was sprawled across the food service table. Patrick—who played Laylo—grabbed some fruit and other snacks as he bragged to another actor in costume. "I got this Donnie cat totally freaked out. He don't know whether he's going or coming."

Hunched over the doughnuts, another actor in island garb stuffed his face as if he hadn't eaten for twenty-four hours.

"Dude, take it easy!" said Laylo. "This stuff's gonna be here all day, okay? *All day*."

With a laugh, Laylo/Patrick walked away.

And Twitty, decked out like an actor in an island costume, lifted his head from his feasting. "It is?" he said. "Sweet!"

Doughnut in hand, Twitty went exploring. He took in the whole production setup and soon found the central video tent.

Inside the tent, monitors revealed images of the various Stevenses throughout the island. On one monitor, Ren was stalking Louis. On another, Louis was stalking a squirrel.

Miles looked into a camera's lens and gave his commentary. "Looks like Ren has picked up the trail!" he informed the audience.

"Here, little squirrel," Louis said on the monitor. "Give Daddy back his peanut." But the squirrel scampered from Louis's grasp—and he screamed in frustration.

On Ren's monitor, the viewers could hear Louis scream off camera. Ren ran toward her annoying brother.

Standing before the camera, Miles promised, "This is gonna be *sweet*!"

"I'll show *you* sweet," Twitty vowed. He walked over to an exposed grid at the rear of the tent. Then he pulled every wire and threw every switch he could find!

Inside the tent, every last monitor went snowy—and Miles went ballistic.

"What's going on!" Miles shouted. "She was just getting ready to nail him!"

Keith and his technicians furiously hit switches and buttons. "Everything's dead!" yelled Keith.

Just out of sight, Twitty smiled and whispered, "Now, *that's* sweet!"

Inside Roller Cakes, *Family Fake-Out!* went off the air. A graphic flashed on the screen: PLEASE STAND BY.

"Oh, man," Tugnut said over a disappointed murmur from the crowd. "It was just getting good."

Another show came on, featuring an attractive dark-haired woman standing in a suburban kitchen with a basket full of eggs.

"Hi, Cynthia Mills here," the woman said. "What could be more festive for the holidays than your own personalized, hand-painted Easter egg?"

"Rip-off!" Tugnut hollered. Everyone in the diner joined in the chant. "Rip-off! Rip-off! Rip-off!"

In the control tent, Miles screamed at the crew: "Get us back on the air!"

Scott and Brooke raced in. "Miles, it's the Twitty kid—" Scott started.

"He's missing!" Brooke finished.

"I *bet* he had something to do with this," Miles said gravely. "You find him!"

"Great idea!" said Scott, ever the chipper toady.

"You always know exactly what to do," Brooke added, not to be out-toadied.

"Go!" yelled Miles. And they went.

Outside the tent, everyone was scrambling and shouting. They had no sound. Communications with the remote crews were lost.

Meanwhile, the grinning and safely disguised Twitty calmly strolled past the frantic rush of technicians, ignoring the actor who hollered, "Hey! Where's my costume?"

* * *

Near the rocky shore, Mrs. Stevens waded into the surf trying to spear a fish with a pointy stick. She shrieked as she backed into her husband, who was doing the same thing.

They brandished their sticks like swords and glared at each other. Then they sighed.

"Truce?" Mr. Stevens asked, offering his little finger.

Mrs. Stevens softened, touched pinkies, and held her husband's hand.

Meanwhile, the ferocious, rabid squirrel was back—chasing Donnie.

Donnie ran into a clearing, brandishing a pair of sticks. Crying out in fear, he gasped as he bumped into—

"Donnie?" Tawny asked.

Donnie jumped back, his brow furrowing. "*Tawny?* What are you doing here?"

He circled her wildly. "No, no, no, no," repeated Donnie. "Not again, not again. You're not cutting class, right?"

"I don't know," Tawny said, rubbing her

head. "I have this horrible headache, and I don't know how I got here."

He clapped a hand on her shoulder and urged her along as he made his way back to the others. "Okay, you're coming with me," he told her.

"Why?" Tawny asked.

"So this time people will believe me!" he cried.

Mr. and Mrs. Stevens strolled along the beach, hand in hand.

"I guess I'm just overly sensitive about this whole job thing," Mr. Stevens admitted.

Mrs. Stevens raised an eyebrow. "Well, the fact that we're starving on an island in the middle of nowhere might have something to do with it, too," she told him.

"This couldn't have been a worse vacation if someone had planned it this way," Mr. Stevens said.

As soon as he said it, they stopped and stared at each other as the exact same thought occurred to both of them: *Maybe somebody did!*

As Beans met up with them, all three began to compare notes.

"So, Miles gave you the impression that we wanted all the food?" Mr. Stevens asked his wife.

"Yes," she told him. "And when we got there everything was empty."

"Same with us," Mr. Stevens said. "So what happened to it?"

"There never was any food or I would have smelled it," Beans assured them.

Mr. Stevens sighed. "You know what? I think he would have."

"Do you think Miles knew?" asked Mrs. Stevens.

Mr. Stevens shook his head. "I don't know," he said. "It seemed like he was always trying to help us."

They passed a few stone idols and emerged from the woods. Mrs. Stevens pondered, "Yeah, but every time he tried to help us, things got worse."

Donnie appeared and pointed at Tawny. "Okay, how do you explain this?" he demanded.

"Tawny?" Mrs. Stevens couldn't believe her eyes.

"What are *you* doing here?" Mr. Stevens asked.

"I don't know," Tawny said.

Donnie turned to Tawny. "*That's* why I'm asking, 'How do you explain this?'"

Tawny frowned. "Okay, there was something I had to tell Louis," she said.

Mrs. Stevens looked around. "Where's Louis?" she asked.

"And Ren," Mr. Stevens added.

"Hey, guys, look what I found!" Beans cried, pulling up a length of cable from the dirt. Everyone charged over and examined it. "I thought this island doesn't get cable," complained Beans.

Donnie scratched his head and agreed, "That's what Miles said. . . ."

Mr. Stevens frowned. "Miles said a lot of things."

"Wait—Miles McDermott?" Tawny asked.

Everyone turned to face her.

"How do you know Miles McDermott?" asked Mrs. Stevens suspiciously.

"It's all coming back to me," said Tawny. "He's on television. He's the host of *Family Fake-Out!*"

"Never heard of it," said Beans.

"You haven't? It's the hottest new show," Tawny told them. "Everybody watches it."

"We don't," said Donnie.

"You don't?" Tawny looked around, working something out in her head. Then it came to her. "Of course not, because you're *on* it right now. There are cameras watching you everywhere you go."

Stunned, everyone automatically scanned the area for cameras.

"It makes sense now," Mrs. Stevens realized. "This was all a setup!"

Donnie called out, "Okay, everybody watching out there: I knew about it all along!"

"Miles! Miles, this is not funny!" Mrs. Stevens cried as she smacked the belly of an idol with the tropical flower she'd been carrying. "This is cruel and humiliating!"

Mr. Stevens joined the others. "Okay, joke's over! You can come out and have a good laugh now!"

Beans started laughing uproariously at them. Mr. Stevens's gaze narrowed. "Not *you*," he snapped.

"Okay," Mrs. Stevens said. "Where is everybody?"

As far as the Stevenses were concerned, the search was just beginning. Their tormentors could run—but they could no longer hide!

Miles waded through the mass of frantic technicians working to get them back on the air.

"How long does it take to reconnect a few lousy cable wires?" Miles demanded throwing his hands in the air.

Enraged, he pointed at one technician after another. "You're fired! You're fired! You're fired! You're all fired," he cried. Then he stormed off, pointing at extras and crew at random. "Who are you? You're fired. Fired! FIRED!"

Mr. and Mrs. Stevens, Donnie, Beans, and Tawny all began to walk through the woods. They left the thick greenery and came to a lake with a gentle waterfall in the distance. It was such a pretty day and such a pretty place—and that made it hard for everyone to believe they were in the midst of something so ugly and cruel.

"There is no Mandelino," Tawny explained. "You're on Catalona."

"That's right off the coast," realized Mr. Stevens. "I feel like such a *jerk*."

"Now you know how I felt when I told you about Patrick Green," Donnie said glumly.

"Oh, you're so right, son," Mrs. Stevens assured him. "I'm sorry. If we had believed you, it would have saved all this trouble."

"Hey guys, over there!" Beans called. He pointed to an islander sauntering by in a long grass skirt and an elaborate headdress.

"I bet he knows where Miles is," Mrs. Stevens said excitedly. "Don't let him get away!"

Donnie took off—the family at his heels—and *tackled* the guy. Everyone crowded around and stared down at the fallen actor.

"Okay, where is he?" Donnie asked.

"Where's who?" the actor asked.

Then Donnie stopped and stared at the actor's familiar face. "Twitty?"

117

Twitty looked up at the sea of Stevenses above him. "I'm really sorry," Twitty said earnestly. "Do you guys hate me?"

"Alan, we could never hate you," Mrs. Stevens said sweetly. Then she whacked him with her exotic flower. "What did you do?"

"Nothin'. Just came by to help," Twitty said. He cleared his throat. "After I sold you guys out."

Donnie's eyes widened. "So you know we're on TV?" he asked.

Twitty smiled and informed them, "Actually, right now—you're *not*."

Twitty led Tawny, Beans, Donnie, and Mr. and Mrs. Stevens to a hillock with a view of the valley housing the production's base camp.

They all stared at the flurry of activity below them. Shaking their heads, they watched as crew members and costumed actors rushed around.

Twitty smiled with pride. "They should be off the air for a little while," he said. "I did some serious scrambling down there."

"That's good, that's good," Mrs. Stevens said. "Because, as embarrassing as this was for us, we still have a chance to show them that they didn't win. That this is a family that sticks together."

"Right. So you forgive me?" asked Twitty.

Mrs. Stevens frowned. "I didn't say that."

"Twitty," Mr. Stevens spoke up, "what was the last thing people saw on TV?"

"You scratching yourself with a stick . . . for a long time. . . ." Twitty told him.

"What *else*?" asked Mr. Stevens.

"Beans was smelling a beetle . . ." Twitty reminisced. "Oh, and Ren was trying to kill Louis."

Everyone's jaw dropped at that last item.

Beans was the only one not impressed. In his lifetime, he'd already seen Ren trying to kill Louis too many times to count.

"So are we gonna get these suckers, or what?" Beans asked the group.

"Oh, we're gonna get them," Mr. Stevens assured him. "But first, we've got to get to Ren and Louis. Come on!"

119

Miles gripped the golf cart's steering wheel as he sped across the production area. Scott and Brooke were with him, frantically scribbling notes.

"I want to know who was guarding that Twitty kid!" Miles yelled. "And how he got into the video truck!"

Keith rushed over as the cart came to a stop. "We've got picture! We can go back on the air," he informed Miles.

Miles rocketed from the cart. "All right, people! Let's go! Let's go!" he cried.

"You don't *have* any people," Keith reminded him. "You fired everyone."

Miles pointed at the technicians. "You're rehired! You're rehired! You're rehired!" he told them. Then he rushed toward the control booth. "If there's any justice in this world, Ren hasn't caught up with Louis yet. Come on, let's go! Get them on camera."

At Roller Cakes, Tugnut was in the middle of taking notes about how to paste little paper ears onto his Easter eggs.

"Now, your eggs will want to have a pair of little *bunny* ears!" Cynthia Mills cooed on the TV screen. "And now you can hear me say how cute you are!"

There was an eruption of static—and Miles reappeared on the screen. "Hey, we're back," he announced. "Sorry for those technical difficulties, but that's what makes a live show so *exciting*."

"What about the bunny ears?" cried Tugnut.

Larry stepped up behind him and chided, "Coach!"

Embarrassed, Tugnut recovered to his macho self. "I mean—thank goodness *that's* over," he said with a grunt.

"Before our little break, Louis was hunting a squirrel and Ren was hunting Louis," Miles said to the camera.

But when Miles turned to the monitors in the control tent, there was no sign of Ren or Louis. Miles turned to his director. From the corner of his mouth he hissed, "Keith, where are those kids?"

"I don't know," Keith admitted.

Miles put on a show for the camera. "Well, this might be a good time to examine the natural beauty of the island. The flowers, the trees . . ."

"We found 'em!" Keith called.

"Later for nature," Miles snapped. "Let's get back to the action."

A hand thrust a stone against the edge of a stick, sharpening it into a deadly spear. A face loomed beside it. Gleeful. Savage. Streaked with war paint.

It was Ren. She tested the sharpened point with relish. "Ohhhh, Louis," she growled, "I *know* you're out there!"

Watching from his broadcasting tent, Miles gulped at the drastic and disturbing change in the lovely, intelligent Ren.

"Looks like Ren is ticked off," Miles said to the viewers at home. "I wouldn't want to be Louis right now!"

Meanwhile, miles away, in Ruby's bedroom, Monique was beside herself. "Ren has totally lost it," she cried, pointing at the TV screen.

Ruby frowned. "No, not Ren. She's always in control."

The girls watched as Ren unleashed a blood-curdling scream—and then *hissed* like a snake.

On the TV screen, Miles laughed nervously as the cameras cut back to him.

"Wow, there's a lot of rage there," he said, his face betraying traces of worry.

The camera panned to Louis, who was scrambling on his hands and knees, following a trail through the woods.

Desperate with hunger, he mumbled something about the soft squishy center of squirrels and how the little guy could keep an arm or leg, he wasn't greedy—just starved!

123

Ren burst from behind a tree and plunged her spear into the ground before her startled brother.

"Hi, Ren," he croaked. But this *wasn't* Ren. Not the Ren he knew. She wasn't clean. She wasn't preppy. Or perky. Nope, this was some crazy savage with murder in her heart.

Better stay with the squirrel, Louis decided. Smaller, no spear. Staying on his knees, Louis spun away.

"I really liked Mootai," Ren said, raising her spear and pointing it at Louis. "But you just couldn't stand to see me happy!"

"Ren, what are you talking about?" Louis asked.

Circling before him like a jungle cat, Ren rammed the spear down once more, making Louis flinch.

"You ruined my life!" Ren snarled.

"When?" asked Louis.

Ren knelt and thrust her face close to that of her scared little brother. "The day you were *born*!"

"Ren—your shoe's on fire!" Louis hollered.

She looked down at her sandal. "Huh?"

Louis scrambled to his feet and bolted!

"You can run," Ren said, aiming her spear as she posed like a huntress, "but you can't hide!"

Then she let out another scream—and tore after her prey!

In Roller Cakes, Larry stared at the TV set high over the counter. He could hardly believe his eyes. Ren was chasing Louis through the woods, the spear nearly tagging the annoying little squirt's backside.

"You go, girl!" Larry hollered.

Across the nation, reactions to the scene were wildly different. Ruby and Monique were horrified. So was Principal Wexler. And in the control tent, even Keith was worried.

"Miles, what if she hurts him?" asked the director. "We're responsible for these people."

"Relax, okay?" Miles said with a weak little laugh. "She's *not* gonna hurt him."

Suddenly, Ren's painted face appeared on the monitor in close-up and she cried, "I'm gonna hurt you, Louis!"

125

Then she gave her best warrior princess scream—and sprinted after him again.

Now Miles really *was* worried.

Atop the island's mighty mountain, Ren spurred—or speared—Louis higher and higher. They burst from cover, and Ren changed her grip on the spear, aiming it with a single hand like a hunter from some savage and long-forgotten age.

"This is it, Louis," Ren said, delirious with the promise of revenge. "There's nowhere left to run!"

Meanwhile, back at Roller Cakes, Coach Tugnut was impressed. "This is better than wrestling!" he yelled. The crowd cheered.

On the TV screen, Ren poked Louis with her spear. Her brother had driven her to the edge plenty of times. Now it was *her* turn. She continued to force Louis toward the cliffside. He looked over the edge to the rocky shore below. It was a *long* way down.

"Okay, Ren, stop! Stop! Enough!" Louis pleaded.

"I can't tell you how long I've been waiting for this day," Ren told him, relishing her position.

"Wait a little bit longer. Please!" he begged.

Screeching tires sounded and clouds of earth rose up as Miles braked his jeep and jumped out. "Hey, kids! Great news," he said. "I just spoke to the tribal elders. They've decided to forgive your family."

Louis brightened. "You hear that, Ren?" he asked with desperation. "See? Everything's great now, that's great news! See? All's well that ends well, right?"

"The only thing that's going to end is *you!*" Ren promised darkly. She shoved the spear closer, jamming it right in her brother's face.

"Ren!" Louis cried. "You know I'm afraid of heights . . . and *spears.*"

Donnie, Mr. and Mrs. Stevens, and Beans rushed over. Mrs. Stevens's hands flailed. "Ren! Louis! We've been looking all over for you," she shouted.

"Ren, what are you doing?" Mr. Stevens yelled.

"I'm about to solve the Louis problem," Ren snarled as she shredded her brother's shirt with her spear.

"I'm glad you're all here," Miles said. "Ren's a little upset. But this is a perfect time to tell you that you're on a reality show called *Family Fake-Out!*"

"Yeah, that's a nice try, Miles," Ren ranted. "But it's *too* late! We're a million miles from nowhere. And if one of us disappeared— *nobody would know*!"

"*I'd* know," Louis informed her meekly. She swiped the spear at his face, making him flinch.

"Ren, Miles is telling the truth," Mrs. Stevens hollered. "It's just a silly TV show."

"I don't believe you!" shouted Ren.

"Ren, listen, please!" Donnie cried. "We just found out. We've been trying to find you guys to tell you!"

"You know, I know what you're doing," Ren railed. "You're trying to protect Louis. You're *always* trying to protect Louis. Well, you know what? I can't take it anymore!"

"No! Ren, no!" Louis hollered.

With a savage scream, Ren poked at him with the spear—and Louis fell backward.

"*Ahhhhhhh!*" Louis screamed as he plunged over the edge, toward the rocky shore.

Chapter 13

"**N**oooo!" shouted the horrified Miles as he sank to his knees.

"My baby!" cried Mrs. Stevens.

"Miles!" Mr. Stevens shouted. "This is all your fault!"

Miles let out a scream of genuine horror and fell to his knees. "I'm so sorry," he sobbed. "It wasn't supposed to end this way. Nobody was supposed to get hurt!"

Miles was losing it. He could not believe what had just happened. And it was all his fault!

Lucky for him, fate cut his suffering short. To Mile's astonishment, a helicopter majestically rose from the abyss.

A handsome man leaned out of the helicopter and spoke into a megaphone. "Miles McDermott, this is Lance Lebow, and I just dropped in to say, *Gotcha!* . . . on your *own* show!"

"Yeah!" Mrs. Stevens shouted.

Miles was flabbergasted. "But . . . Louis?" he squeaked.

Lance gestured to the pilot, and the helicopter lifted up, revealing Louis hanging from a rope ladder.

"Hey, Miles!" Louis hollered. "Hey!"

Miles shuddered. "How did . . . ?"

Louis grinned. "Jumped into a big 'ole net. Just like we planned it."

Tawny and Twitty appeared, carrying a huge net.

"Nice catch, guys," Louis called to the pair. He looked at his sister. "Very convincing, sis."

"Had a lot of practice, bro," Ren said.

"*Gotcha!*" Louis hollered at Miles.

At Roller Cakes, the customers applauded and laughed. Even Larry was smiling. "I gotta admit—that was pretty cool."

Tugnut wiped the sweat from his pale face. "Aw, they didn't fool me for one second," he lied.

On screen, Miles did his best to recover. "Okay," he said, "I think we've had enough *fun* for one day. Why don't we get back to that Easter thing that we were having so much fun with."

Lance eased into the frame and put his arm around Miles. "Or you can flip the channel and watch us live on *Gotcha!*" he quickly suggested.

Miles drew the "cut" sign over his throat and the Cynthia Mills show popped back on. Cynthia was placing a cotton ball on a bunny egg. "A little bunny tail on his little bunny bum!" Cynthia said perkily.

At Roller Cakes, Larry reached up and changed the channel. *Gotcha!* appeared on screen.

"For those of you just tuning in," Lance

continued, "let's hear how we made a total fool out of my old friend Miles on his own show!"

Stuck on camera, Miles forced a smile. "Is this really necessary?" he snapped.

Mrs. Stevens chimed in. "It's necessary. You see Miles, we may argue sometimes, but it takes a lot more than a cheesy TV show to rip this family apart."

"Yeah, right on!" cried Beans.

"Yeah!" yelled Donnie. "Yeah, we figured out everything, Miles. Except the Fire God. How did you get Oprah to turn against us?"

"It's okay, sweetheart," Mrs. Stevens said, patting her son on the shoulder. "We're gonna get you some nourishment."

Lance laughed, then said, "You know, we put this prank together in a matter of just a couple of hours, thanks to family friends Alan Twitty and Tawny Dean."

Lance moved with his cameraman over to Twitty and Tawny. "Now . . . what prompted you two to call *Gotcha!* on your cell phone with this great prank?" he asked.

"Guilt and shame," Twitty said seriously.

133

Tawny raised a finger to the camera. "I would just like to say that embarrassing innocent people on TV for fun and profit is one of the lowest—"

"Okay!" Lance said, pulling Tawny away from the camera.

"Will you let me finish?" Tawny hollered. But she was soon out of the frame again.

Lance's good-natured laugh returned. "Okay, thank you, kids," he said quickly. "Now, Miles, I bet you're wondering how the Stevens family turned the tables on you?"

"No, not really," Miles said through a tight smile. "I've got to get back to the studio."

"What for?" Lance asked. "Your career's over!"

Miles's face dropped. "That's true," he said.

Mr. Stevens jumped in. "You see, people," he began, "when we found Ren, she had Louis trapped in a tree convinced that he was the cause of everything that went bad on this island. When we told the kids it was a setup, they put aside their differences and we all came up with this little charade. Hey, Lance! Get a shot of those little scamps, will ya? Aren't they lovable?"

The *Gotcha!* camera moved to get Ren and Louis in the frame. Ren smiled and waved sheepishly. Louis lifted his shorts to show his white leg.

"Stop!" Ren hollered. "Louis!"

Then the camera swung back to the rest of the family.

"Can I go now?" Miles asked meekly.

"Sure," Donnie promised. "I'll give you a three-second head start."

Miles smiled—then realized the football player was dead serious. He took off as Donnie began counting.

"Remember, folks, watch us next week on—" Lance began.

"*Gotcha!*" everyone cried. Then they took off—to *get* Miles!

Later that day, Ren sat outside, looking out at the beautiful blue water of the Catalona beach. She was freshly showered and dressed in nice, clean clothes. In many ways, she was her old self again . . . but her old self was lonely and a little sad. She barely looked up as Louis approached.

"Hey, Ren. The plane's here," Louis told her. "You ready to go?"

"Uh . . . yeah. I guess so," Ren said unhappily.

He sat down beside her. "You okay?"

"Sure," Ren said, but it wasn't very convincing.

"Okay," said Louis, concerned.

"Look," she told him. "I'm really sorry about blaming you . . . for everything."

"Ren, I'm your brother. I love messing with you. But I would never do anything to hurt you," he assured her.

"I know," Ren said, and she meant it. "Hey, we made a pretty good team, though."

"We made an awesome team," Louis said, high-fiving her. "The all-stars. We had Miles crying like a baby."

"Well, it's gonna be the highlight of my summer," Ren said, smiling through her sadness.

"Summer's not over," Louis reminded her. "You might be able to meet a nice guy or something. Huh?"

"No. I'm not having that much luck in that department," Ren replied.

"Forget about luck," said Louis. "What about Jason?"

"Who?" asked Ren.

"Jason." Louis struck a muscle-man pose, then called out, "Jason!"

The handsome actor who'd played the role of Mootai emerged from behind some nearby trees.

"He's a nice guy," Louis said. "Tend to your business. Talk to him. Later." Then Louis was gone.

Jason came over and sat down. "Ren, I am so sorry about all this . . ." he began.

"It's okay," Ren said, but she was obviously uncomfortable. "You're an actor. You know, it's your job. You were *doing* your job. And you tried to warn me."

"The thing is, I wasn't acting," Jason confessed.

Ren wrinkled her brow. "What does that mean?" she asked.

"I really care about you," Jason said.

They looked into each other's eyes.

"Ren! We're leaving!" called Mr. Stevens.

"I gotta go," Ren said.

"Can I see you again?" Jason asked.

Ren got to her feet, hesitated—then leaned down and kissed him. "You can take that as a *yes*," she assured him with a smile.

And, as she rushed off, Jason smiled too.

The Stevens family and their friends—Beans, Tawny, and Twitty—were farther down the shore, getting ready to board the seaplane. Louis rushed over to his sister.

"Did you say good-bye to Jason?" he asked.

"Yeah. For now. Hey—*thank you*," she said sincerely. "You know, this time you didn't ruin things so bad."

She hugged him tightly. Grinning, Louis kissed her cheek.

"All right, too much love," Louis lamented

after a few moments. Then he turned and yelled, "Everybody get on the plane, let's go. Bring Mom and Dad. Come on, come on!"

"Hey, if there's not enough room, I could swim home," Twitty offered guiltily.

"Don't worry, Twitty, we forgive you," Donnie said.

Twitty's eyes widened. "Really?"

"Yeah, but you're sitting with Beans," Louis said.

Beans put one hand on his stomach. "I'm feeling a little gassy," he said. "I hope the window's open."

Twitty sighed as he moved toward the plane. His punishment awaited—and it stunk!

Louis nodded to Tawny and tried that favorite line of his on her again. "Want to sit right here next to Poppa?"

Tawny shrugged and came his way.

Mr. and Mrs. Stevens took one last look at the island. "Boy, it really could have been beautiful," Mrs. Stevens said.

Mr. Stevens grinned at his wife. "I think it *was*," he said, certain that no matter how many years went by, the Stevens family would never, ever forget *this* vacation.

Mr. Stevens kissed his wife and they climbed aboard.

"How We Spent Our Summer Vacation"
by Beans Arengueren

Donnie went off to college, where he excelled in football, baseball, and philosophy.

Just kidding about the philosophy.

Mr. Stevens got a new job at a great law firm. Yep, Mr. Stevens was bringing home the bacon again. (Unfortunately, that's just an expression.)

Louis got back to his Ultra-Lounge-O-Matic Super Chair, which he shared with Tawny. While Ren and Mootai—whose real name is Jason—became inseparable. I'm talkin' smooches everywhere.

Yuck!

As for me, I spent plenty of quality time with my favorite family. Yep, it was a dream vacation. . . .

With plenty of bacon!

THE END

FIRST TIME ON DVD AND VIDEO

Sassy, Stylish and Psychic!

FEATURES NEVER-BEFORE-SEEN EPISODE

that's so raven

Supernaturally Stylish

COMING DECEMBER 7